ACE OF HEARTS
LIGHT ME UP SERIES - BOOK TWO

D J COOK

H.A. ROBINSON

ACE OF HEARTS

Copyright © 2024 Ace Of Hearts by D J Cook & H.A. Robinson

All rights reserved.

Editor: H.A. Robinson

Cover Design: Shower Of Schmidt Designs

Formatting: D J Cook

No part of this book may be reproduced in any form or by any electronic or mechanical means, including information storage and retrieval systems, without written permission from the author, except for the use of brief quotations in a book review.

Ace Of Hearts is a work of fiction. Names, characters, businesses, places, events and incidents are either the products of the author's imagination or used in a fictitious manner. Any resemblance to actual persons, living or dead, or actual events is purely coincidental.

This book is dedicated to my co-author, H.A. Robinson. I know how much writing this and Lola's story mattered to you and I feel so lucky to have shared the journey with you.

Not only that, but I'm honoured and privileged to call you my friend.

Love, D J Cook xoxo

ACKNOWLEDGMENTS

Ace of Hearts was a must-write book for me, H.A. Robinson. I mentioned to D J Cook one day that I dreamed of writing a book with an ace main character. I assumed he'd nod and smile and say, "Yeah, you should totally do that, one day." Naturally, he didn't. Instead, he jumped at the chance to write this most personal of stories with me. For this, and for a thousand other things, I will be forever indebted to him.

There are so many people to whom we both owe our thanks for their help with this novel.

Eleanor Lloyd Jones, despite working what seems like twenty jobs all at once, still your generosity and expertise flow freely in this book world of ours. Thank you so much for the hours of your own time you've devoted to creating the perfect cover for Ace of Hearts, and creating all the graphics to go with it.

We have been blessed, once again, with an incredible group of beta readers who gave up their time freely and willingly, at the last minute, to give us much-needed feedback. Riah, Emma, Andrea, Blaire and Kristina—we could not do this without you. Your honest feedback is invaluable to us, and we count ourselves as unbelievably lucky to have all of you.

To Evan, thank you for all your love, writing company and motivation (even if sometimes you do like to encourage us to take undeserving breaks to watch TV with you). You're a rock for us both and we love and thank you for your constant support.

To Mama and Papa Ross, thank you for always championing all of our work, for being constant cheerleaders and for your endless love and support. We love you lots and lots like jelly tots!

And lastly, to our angels, Erica and Emma, our guiding lights in the sky—we love you, we miss you, we hope we make you proud. Always.

CHAPTER 1
LOLA

Normal.

It was a word I'd skirted around my entire life. I'd never really known quite what it meant or why I didn't feel like it included me. All I knew was that I didn't feel the same as everybody else. There was always something, just beneath the surface of my skin, that marked me out as different. At least in my own head.

Maybe everybody secretly felt that way. I wasn't sure. All I knew was that if everybody else felt the same way as me, they hid it far better than I did.

That morning, though, as I stood in front of the mirror, squinting at my reflection in distaste, I felt a little more like every other sixteen-year-old girl in the country getting ready for their first day at sixth form. Surely every single one of us was having an existential crisis over their appearance in a mirror on that particular morning.

I was excited and nervous in equal measure, and most of the nerves stemmed from the fact that my partner in crime was going to a different college. It was completely unfair that we wouldn't be haunting the halls of Sandford together anymore. If you asked me, it was pretty shitty that Mr 'Big Balls' Richards wouldn't allow Ollie to stay on just because of his GCSE results. You'd think he'd have cut him some slack after he'd had a massive breakdown and almost shuffled off this mortal coil a good seventy years too early, but no. Apparently, rules were rules, and knobheads were knobheads, and that was that.

So, Ollie was off to Allerton and I'd have to suffer two more years at Sandford without him.

This was going to suck.

At least we could walk part of the way together, but Ollie's twitchy nerves only served to make me worry more about him and his own first day when he deposited me at the Sandford gates and went off on his own.

I doubted there would ever be a day when I wouldn't worry about him. It was like part of my job description by that point.

"Well, if it isn't Lola-Little-Legs," a familiar voice crooned in my ear as an arm landed over my shoulders.

I smiled in spite of myself. Noah Larson was an idiot, but he was kind of an adorable one.

"I could still take you out, Larson, no matter how little my legs might be."

He grinned and we fell into step beside one another, walking towards the familiar building that had been our prison for five years. Now, though, it was different. Now, we got ID cards that could scan us in and out of the building whenever we felt like it. Apparently, we were basically miniature adults now, which meant we could be trusted to take responsibility for our own learning. If we missed a lesson and elected to go to Costa instead, that was on us. Nobody would be chasing us up now. It was all on us.

The thought was equal parts terrifying and liberating.

"So, how was the summer?" Noah asked as we strode into the sixth form area side-by-side. The building was ancient—made of the same old, crumbled red brick as the rest of the school, but to us, it felt like walking into a palace made of gold. This was the hallowed ground we'd been forbidden from setting foot on for the last five years, and now it was our kingdom.

"Oh, you know…" I shrugged, not really wanting to go into detail about how I'd spent most of the summer worrying about Ollie and hanging out with him, watching Heartstopper over and over because it seemed to help him to feel better for some weird reason only he could have explained. "Quiet. How was yours?"

His blue eyes shone as he launched into a detailed account of his summer surfing the beaches of Cornwall with his older brother. I watched him talking, his hands gesticulating wildly as he grew more animated, his blond hair dropping over his eyes, making him look every inch the surfer.

I wouldn't have traded my summer with Ollie for the world after we'd come so close to losing him, but a part of me couldn't help feeling jealous of Noah's summer adventures, even if I did hate the idea of setting foot in the ocean.

"It sounds amazing," I said when he finished, unable to keep a slight note of wistfulness out of my voice.

"It really was," he agreed, nudging my chin with his

finger and smiling widely. "You should come with us next time."

With that, he released me from my position under his arm and walked off to greet the others whose group Ollie and I had always been on the peripheries of.

They were all there. Everybody had returned except for Ollie—my wingman and magnetic north. Standing there, surrounded by all the people I'd known for so long, while reunions, hugs and laughter filled the air, my arms tugged my jacket a little tighter around me as a lost feeling swelled up inside my chest.

I was part of it, but not really. Everybody had their person within the group that they gravitated towards more than anybody else. Everybody except me, now.

My hands twitched to reach for my phone to message Ollie, but I needed to push that urge down. He would have his life at Allerton, and I needed to forge forwards with mine here. Ollie was forever telling me I was a 'people person', so I guessed now was time to put that theory to the test.

Moving into the circle of enthusiastic reunions, I forced a massive grin onto my face and shuffled towards Evie, a girl I'd always been casually friendly with. My stomach cramped, hoping when I went in for the hug, she wouldn't reject it, or me, outright. My muscles relaxed, though, when she accepted the hug readily enough and cheerfully chatted to me about her summer visiting her mum's family in Jamaica, and asked the usual questions about mine.

Then, inevitably, her head tilted in that way that always told you the serious question was coming. "Hey, how's Ollie? Is he doing okay now?"

I matched her head tilt with the expected small but genuine smile, and nodded. "He's doing... better. He got into Allerton so he's doing his A levels there."

"Oh, that's great. It was so crap what happened."

I secretly thought crap was a pretty ineffective word to describe the day I'd received a text from my best friend in the world that simply read *I'm sorry*. And 'crap' definitely didn't cover the feeling of hunting around the school site and then around the entire area only to get a phone call from his mum telling me she'd found him lying in a pool of his own blood in the bathroom with a razor blade still clutched in his hand.

"Yeah. Yeah, it was really crap," I agreed, because nobody wanted those details. It was enough for most people just to know it had happened. They didn't need to know how finding out your best friend didn't want to live anymore could tear your soul into pieces that it was almost impossible to fit back together.

"So," I went on, eager to change the subject. "Tell me more about Jamaica. It sounds amazing."

CHAPTER 2
NOAH

Normal.

My summer holiday had been just like the previous four. The minute my brother had graduated we'd found any excuse to make the most of the camper van he'd bought and spruced up with his student loans. Now that Nate was a boring maths teacher at Allerton High, it meant that his holidays could be spent doing what we loved. Summer was the perfect opportunity to get away and feel like a normal teenager without the pressures of life.

The summer vibes quickly diminished, though, as I helped my brother unload the surfboards from the camper only a few days before the start of sixth form. No more adrenaline pumping through my body. No more spray from the ocean as I pushed the board deeper into the waves. Back to books and lessons and all the things you are meant to escape from in summer.

The only thing I had to look forward to was seeing my friends. I'd barely seen my best friend all summer, although even if I hadn't been away, I knew full well that Sam would have been stuck in front of his games console for the entire break. He found much more joy in topping up his screen tan and playing games with randoms online than going outside and playing a game of footy in the fresh air. Who knew playing FIFA could be more appealing than the actual sport?

And then there was Lola.

I'd known Lola ever since our first days at Sandford High School. I'd watched her sit in our tutor group, three rows in front of me, nervous and inseparable from her best friend, Ollie, who she'd known long before her time at high school. Since then, I'd seen her grow into this small but mighty force, a beautiful young woman I called my friend. But god, I wished for more.

With Ollie around, I'd always found it quite difficult to get a look in with Lola. They'd always seemed to be almost literally joined at the hip, but according to the Sandy Crew group chat that had kept us all in gossip over the summer, Ollie was bound for Allerton Sixth Form. That was where my brother taught, which meant I might finally stand a chance of spending some time with Lola.

I slammed my hand down on my phone to silence the blaring alarm that rang down my ear, and sat up, rubbing my eyes as they adjusted to the light that had crept in through the crack in the curtains.

Summer was officially over, though I knew I'd continue to dream about being back on my board and surfing the waves. Without fail, my daydreams always transported me back to my favourite place in the world.

With no more hesitation, I embraced the start of a new

day and flung my curtains wide open. Within twenty minutes I had styled my blond hair, got dressed and wolfed down my breakfast before meeting Sam outside the park to walk to the school together.

"Wassup, bro?" Sam said, his voice deeper than ever.

"Woah. Since when did your balls drop? And when did you start calling me bro?" I laughed, teasing him. He was paler than usual, no doubt due to lack of sunlight and Vitamin D, but credit where it was due… he'd come off his game long enough to get ready for his first day and he had managed to be on time.

"I dunno." He shrugged. "Thought it was a cool thing to say. The lads say it all the time on chat. And where and how my balls are positioned is none of your concern." Sam smirked as we began our walk to school, taking the same route we had for the last five years.

"If you say so. *Bro.*"

Sam and I met a couple of other friends on the way into sixth form but not the one person my eyes eagerly scanned for in the distance. It was only when we approached the school gates that I saw her distinctive pitch-black ponytail. I ran ahead of the gang, fighting with the nervous twitch in my stomach that grew stronger the closer I got to her.

After not seeing her all summer, I had to start by calling her by her nickname. I'd called her Lola-Little-Legs since I'd noticed she'd stopped growing in year nine. It was the one thing guaranteed to get a reaction from her and hadn't failed me since we'd become friends. I'd always remember the time we went on a school trip to Alton Towers and she was too small to go on the rides. Her face was all screwed up as she stood next to the height restriction board until I called her 'Lola-Little-Legs'. All our friends gasped, but not her—her expression softened immediately, followed swiftly by an almighty punch in my right arm and my favourite thing about her—her wit. She had a remark for almost everything.

God, I'd missed her.

Before long, we all had our ID cards and headed towards the side of the school marked as off limits for all students except years twelve and thirteen.

Despite my best failed efforts to try to sneak in, the sixth form common room somehow seemed familiar, likely from hearing Nate talk so fondly about his sixth form memories.

The common room even had the same old coffee machine, covered in markings of past students inscribed into the chrome, which had somehow survived all the years of abuse from caffeine deprived teenagers. I searched the machine and found Nate's name in the exact spot he'd told me to look, so I snapped a picture and sent it to him.

I pressed the cup icon on the machine and listened to it howl and moan as it struggled to brew a single cup of coffee. And after tasting it, I had all the regrets.

"Urgh. That's not coffee. It tastes like rusty tap water." I groaned in distaste.

"I can't believe you even used it. Everyone knows the coffee machine is an ancient heirloom, handed down from year to year." The coffee machine had become a bit of a leaving tradition with students, who'd all etched their names into it on their last day. "Use the kettle instead. Anyway, there are loads of coffee shops around the corner. That's what free periods were made for," Sam said, looking down at his brand new timetable. We only had one lesson together because Sam had opted for all things computer and geek related. I, on the other hand, had picked a wide variety of subjects because I had no idea what I wanted to do. I'd chosen history, geography, economics and IT to cover all grounds.

The bell rang and with a quick wave goodbye to Sam, I was off to class. "See you after lunch in IT."

First lesson of the day was geography and I struggled to shake off that summer feeling, gazing at the classroom displays that Miss Hunt had lovingly put together, apparently spending the majority of her summer in the classroom rather than having a break.

With a single glance at the display board for coastal erosion, I was transported right back to Cornwall, daydreaming about the ocean breeze and the taste of salt water as my surfboard crashed against the waves.

"Psst," someone whispered, stealing away the idyllic feeling that rushed through my body.

"Huh, what?" I said in hushed tones to Alfie who was sitting behind me, rocking on the hind legs of his chair.

"I'm having a party Friday night. You're coming, right?" he said with a smile. I'd wondered how long it would be before he had one of his parties. To be fair, throwing great parties was likely his only talent, other than pulling girls.

"Who's invited?" I asked.

"Everyone. The more the merrier."

"Alfie, can you please pay attention and stop organising your *cool kids back to school party* please? You may think you're being quiet, but in fact it's all the whole class has listened to, despite my attempts to run through the curriculum for your first year of geography A-level."

Miss Hunt was the type of teacher I imagined my brother to be.

Firm but fair.

Down with the kids but didn't take any BS.

"Sorry, Miss." Alfie's chair rocked forward, planting all four legs firmly on the ground. "Love your display boards by the way," he said with an innocent flicker of his eyelashes, a comment sweet enough to make Miss Hunt blush with a glowing smile as she continued her lesson.

Not that I remembered much of it. All I remembered afterwards was spending most of the lesson mentally running through different ways I could ask Lola to go to Alfie's party with me.

The nerves continued to grow in my stomach the more I thought about it, so I decided the minute I saw her, I'd ask her.

What was the worst that could happen?

I shrugged off thoughts of her punching me in the face and ruining a friendship that had spanned five years, and instead counted down the minutes until the next time I'd see her.

CHAPTER 3
LOLA

It was inevitable, I suppose, that I'd lose my phone at some point during the day when I was compulsively checking it for SOS messages from Ollie. I'd heard nothing by period three, Health and Social Care, when I got caught slipping my phone out to check it and Mrs Leary pounced on it like a lion on its prey.

She'd always hated me.

So now I had no way to find out whether Ollie was okay until the end of the day.

It was fine. I was fine. I was sure he was fine. Everything was definitely fine.

The lesson was pointless anyway. *An Introduction to Health and Social Care: What the course is about.* It was about health and it was about social care. Obviously.

If you were going to sacrifice your phone to the confiscation gods, you should at least make it worth it. I was fuming.

At least I was sitting next to somebody I knew, though. I hadn't really had Evie down as a health and social care kind of girl. I'd had her pegged as a definite full-on four difficult A-levels person, but it turned out she wanted to be a children's nurse, and I was glad of the company of somebody I knew and got along with.

It must have been nice to be so sure of what you wanted to do. I still had no idea. All I knew was that I wanted a job that would make a difference to somebody's life. The world could be truly awful sometimes, and most of the time I felt like it was only the little acts of kindness people did for each other that kept the world from imploding in on itself. I was hoping to make a career out of them. I just didn't know how, yet. I'd always been jealous of people who were so focused in one direction. I'd always felt a little like I was being pulled in a million different directions, especially now, in a world where there were so many different people in need of kindness.

By break time, invitations were already circulating around to a party at Alfie Wilson's place.

Alfie was harmless. He liked alcohol and he liked girls. His needs were pretty basic, but if you weren't up for either, he pretty much left you alone.

I couldn't have been less interested. In him. In boys in general. I assumed those particular hormones would kick in at some point and I'd go boy mad like most of my friends had been since we were in year eight of high school, but I was still waiting.

There was definitely something wrong with me, but I tried, not always successfully, not to dwell on it because I had no idea what my issue was or what I could do about it. So, I just kept waiting and hoping.

One day, I was sure I'd want a boyfriend.

Until then, I was willing, if not content, to sit back and watch the antics of my friends. And when it came to Alfie, there was plenty to watch. He didn't see girls so much as potential partners but as conquests to be notched on his bedpost and then disposed of.

His latest target was Summer Geary, a tall, blonde girl with the biggest boobs I'd ever seen on somebody our age. She'd played hard to get for roughly two hours before succumbing to his apparent charms, and now she was his date to the upcoming party at his enormous house on the other side of town.

"You'll come, won't you, Little-Legs?" Noah questioned me at lunchtime, shoving the invite in front of my face as I mainlined my fourth Pepsi Max of the day.

I quirked an eyebrow at him, taking another long drink before slamming the empty can down on the table in front of me and grabbing my cheese sandwich to get started on. "Hadn't really thought about it. I guess it would be a shame to miss out on the final act of the Alfie and Summer show."

"Precisely." He snapped his fingers at me with a grin. "The curtain coming down on that particular shit show is gonna be epic. Summer seems like an absolute psycho and he's definitely gonna break it off the moment he gets what he wants. That's what all the other guys are saying, anyhow. Only one of them is coming out of that mess alive and my money's on Summer."

I chuckled, but glanced over at where Summer and Alfie were curled around each other in the corner of the common room as though they couldn't keep their hands off each other. I studied the pairing curiously, trying to picture myself in her place, but the thought made my skin crawl and I blinked and looked away quickly. Now wasn't the time to focus on my own abnormalities. I doubted there would ever be a good time for that.

"I dunno," I said softly, looking back at Noah who was watching me with interest. "I'm not sure she's a psycho. I think she looks kinda sad most of the time."

"You think?" Noah's eyes widened as he looked back over at the couple who were now trying to suck each other's faces off, totally oblivious to their audience.

"Yeah." I nodded. "She's been through some nasty stuff in her life. She needs somebody who gives a shit about her, and I really don't think that person is Alfie. But, you never know. The leopard might grow stripes one day. Maybe she'll tame him."

Noah nodded thoughtfully, still watching the pair with his head tilted sideways, as though he was seeing them through different eyes than he had only a moment earlier.

"Is it hard work?" he asked, glancing at me and then back over at them.

"Huh?"

"Being such a good person—is it as exhausting as it sounds?"

I laughed, taking a bite of my sandwich and chewing it slowly before replying. "Nah, but when you're perpetually single, you have lots of time to spare to notice stuff about other people. It's a perk." I shrugged and took another bite, trying to ignore the stab of pain in my stomach at the words 'perpetually single'.

Was this me forever? Would I ever start to want what everybody else wanted? Would I ever even develop a crush on somebody? It sounded ridiculous, but even agonising unrequited love would have made me feel a bit better somehow. At least then I would have known I was capable of those sorts of feelings.

"You're not perpetually single," he said with a soft smile. "You just know your own worth and you're not falling for the idiotic horny teenage boy thing. Can't say I blame you, to be honest. We're an appalling breed of human."

I laughed and nudged my shoulder with his. "Nah, some of you aren't so bad."

By the time I got my phone back from a scowling Mrs Leary, coupled with a lecture about how I hadn't even made it through the first day without that 'infernal device', the screen was full of notifications from Ollie.

It was my instinct to panic at the sight of so many messages from him, and I was ready to scream abuse in Mrs Leary's face until I opened up the messages and saw a thread full of memes that had been sent at lunchtime.

Relief was a living thing inside me, taking me from tense panic to relaxed in the flick of a switch.

Would I ever not worry about him?

I relaxed even more when I finally saw him at the school gates. He seemed perfectly cheerful, being dramatic about some lad in his English class who he definitely had a crush on, which he absolutely wouldn't have done if he'd been depressed. His default mode when he was struggling was to shut up shop altogether and not really talk at all. I'd tried like hell to train him out of it over the summer after he'd almost checked out of life altogether, but he was still a nightmare for internalising instead of sharing.

So, the fact he was having a good old moan about his English partner made my heart happy. The fact he'd obviously had a relatively successful first day made me hold my tongue about how much I missed having him around at Sandford. He didn't need to hear how many times throughout the day I'd caught myself sitting in the middle of a crowded room feeling all alone. And I certainly didn't tell him about Alfie's party.

Ollie hated parties.

I was mostly indifferent to them, but they weren't a source of existential panic for me like they were for him.

I'd ride this one out alone. Take one for the team as it were.

I let him chat about his day and how much his new crush irritated him, and kept quiet. Anything to keep him happy.

Anything to keep him.

CHAPTER 4
NOAH

Lola was coming to Alfie's party.

It was a date.

Except, Lola didn't know it was a date. Because I hadn't asked her out like I was supposed to. Because my damn brain and mouth had failed to communicate like they should have done—both having some sort of internal malfunction at the thought of asking Lola out.

But still, Lola was going to be at Alfie's party and although it technically wasn't a mutually understood date, I hoped it would be *the* evening that brought us closer together.

And that hopeful feeling in my chest grew larger and larger as her words repeated in my mind.

"Nah, some of you aren't so bad."

I rubbed where our shoulders had playfully met and couldn't help but grin.

She was right. We weren't all bad; I certainly wasn't—I was going to be the best for her.

Life could sometimes be rocky, and the world was

often an undesirable place to live, but it was never like that around Lola. Her infectious personality was addictive. I couldn't get enough of her. Every minute I spent around her made me want an hour more.

I splashed cold water on my blushing red cheeks, hoping it would douse the nervous fire that had burnt underneath them ever since Lola had agreed to come to Alfie's party with me. It didn't work. Instead, I found myself looking at my reflection in the bathroom mirror. My hair looked as though I'd just fallen off my board into Newquay bay as I watched water drip from my wet, unruly hair and brows.

After the teasing I'd endured from my brother this summer about having a crush on Lola, I just hoped my blotchy red cheeks, lighting up my face like the Blackpool Illuminations, would calm down before our Monday family dinner. I knew it would end up being another occasion for a grilling from my brother who was convinced Lola was my girlfriend.

I wish.

"Noah, Nate's here," Mum yelled up to my room just as the unmistakable smell of Nate's favourite food filled the entire house. Steak and halloumi fajitas, because chicken was bland and boring according to my brother. I had to admit, they were delicious.

"Hey, Noey, come here," he teased, and opened his arms out for a hug. He knew full well the only person allowed to call me Noey was Aunty Joan. Nate was just jealous that I was her favourite and he didn't get a cute nickname.

"Nathaniel." I smirked, patting his back mid hug until

his hand formed a fist to give me a noogie. "Ow. That hurts. Stop. MUMMM!" I yelled.

"Boys, come on now. You are not children anymore. Nate, go lay the table. Noah, come help me in the kitchen," Mum ordered and we both listened, but that didn't stop Nate from sticking his tongue out like a child before disappearing into the dining room. He may have been twenty-five years old but he didn't act it, not at home. I assumed his playfulness was amplified at home because he had to be so sensible at work.

"Smells really good, Mum."

"Ah, thank you. Get me a few serving spoons out of the utensil drawer, would you?" I nodded and was about to walk over to the drawer when Mum stopped me in my tracks. "What's up with your face? Are you warm?" She placed the back of her hand on my forehead but didn't seem concerned about my temperature.

"No, I'm fine. Sam and I ran home. My cheeks have been red since," I lied, knowing full well the only way I'd get Sam to run was by telling him his favourite gaming shop was having a closing down sale.

"Ah," she said with a smile. "How's Lola doing?"

I placed the serving spoons on the kitchen top next to her and muttered, "Fine."

"Oh. That's good."

She didn't say anything else.

Mum's interrogation tactics were much more cruel than the usual shining of a bright light in my eyes. She'd remain quiet, the silence torturing me so much that it forced out word vomit, putting an end to the quiet.

"It was good to see her today. Going to a party with her on Friday night. You know Alfie? He's having another one.

It should be good. The party... Not seeing Lola again. Well..."

"That sounds nice. She's a lovely girl. Pity your father and I don't see her around this way much. She's always with that friend of hers, what's his name?" she asked while popping on an oven glove and carrying the fajita pan into the dining room, resting it on a heat-proof plate Nate had placed out in preparation.

"You mean Ollie? He's not at Sandford anymore. He goes to Allerton, where Nate works."

Nate glanced up from the table where he was sitting in his usual spot. "Ollie? Oh the new sixth-former that started today. Yeah, I heard about him in the staff briefing this morning," Nate said smugly.

"What did you hear? Lola didn't really mention anything to me. Maybe I can talk to her... and help her."

"Nope. Can't tell you, sorry. Student-teacher confidentiality prevents it. Besides, you only want to know to get extra brownie points with your crush," Nate mocked me.

"Come on. It's not like you took a teacher's oath or anything. Spill," I said, trying to get as much halloumi as possible on my spoon while Nate fought to do the same, his spoon clashing against mine.

"No, but there is such a thing as GDPR, dweeb. Stop stealing all the halloumi. That's the best bit."

"Who even says dweeb anymore? God, you're old. And I know it's the best bit; that's why I'm trying to get my share before you take the lot." I pulled a face, just as his spoon clinked mine just a little too hard, causing bright red fajita sauce to splatter up the cream curtains. And Mum walked in just in time to see the whole thing.

"Nathaniel! Noah! I'm sick to death of your incessant

childish behaviour. No wonder neither of you have girlfriends. You should be ashamed of yourselves. Now, if you don't stop with your bickering, you'll go hungry. And save some for me and your father." Right on cue, Mum walked into the kitchen to get her rubber gloves and cleaning products. "I guess I will be eating after I've cleaned the damn curtains."

"Sorry, Mum," we both said simultaneously as the guilt swallowed me up. Our usual brotherly antics had turned the evening upside down for Mum who wouldn't be able to focus on anything until the curtains were spotless, even if it meant going hungry. Nate seemed unfazed by the whole thing as I endured a kick to the shin from Nate, who carried on without a care in the world for our mother.

"How is your girlfriend?" Nate teased in Mum's absence.

"She's not my girlfriend. Do you not have anything better to do on a Monday night?" I glared at Nate.

"Nope. I live for Mondays. What could be better than winding up my ickle-baby brother, Noey?"

"You're such a loser."

Nate wore a sarcastic smile for the rest of the evening, while I spent that time daydreaming about my two favourite things—surfing and Lola—and eagerly awaited our time together on Friday night.

CHAPTER 5

LOLA

There were some girls who just seemed to look effortlessly amazing no matter what they wore or how they did their hair and make-up.

I was not one of those girls.

I generally sported a look that you might call swamp demon on a good day. I had zero fashion sense, and honestly, I didn't really care. Usually

But then inconvenient things like parties came along and suddenly, I felt the pressure to give more of a damn about my appearance. But it didn't matter what I put on or how I tried to style my hair, I still looked like Lola the tomboy, trying too hard to look like Lola the girly girl for one night only.

I was a mess.

But it was the best it was going to get, so I turned away from the mirror and grabbed my bag, ready to go.

"Party time. Woo," I deadpanned to myself, waving in a mock jazz hands as I ran downstairs to where Mum was waiting to drive me to Alfie's. Dave, my loyal cocker spaniel, spun madly around my legs as I pulled my boots on, thinking I was taking him for a walk.

"Sorry, buddy. Not tonight. I'll make it up to you tomorrow, I promise."

Alfie's house was one of the gigantic new builds on the other side of town. I'd arranged to meet Noah outside because neither of us wanted to go in alone. He was there waiting for me when I arrived, standing there in a navy shirt with short sleeves and a pair of black jeans.

His face lit into a massive smile when he spotted me clambering out of my mum's car, and I couldn't deny that it was kind of nice to have somebody other than Ollie be pleased to see me.

"Thought you were standing me up for a minute there," he said with a nervous laugh as he gave me a warm, welcoming hug.

"I had a wardrobe malfunction," I explained with a smile.

"Oh?" He looked me up and down and gave me an approving look. "You sure about that?"

"Oh, absolutely. My entire life is a wardrobe malfunction."

"I respectfully disagree," he said before taking my hand and dragging me playfully into the house.

The moment the door swung open, the music blasted my ears and my heart rate kicked up a notch. I loved music, and the key selling point of parties for me was dancing.

"I love this song," I announced loudly to Noah, who

was divesting me of my coat and shoving it onto a pile by the door.

"Oh, yeah, me too," he replied uncertainly. "Wanna dance?"

Beaming, I accepted the hand he had extended out to me. "I thought you'd never ask."

The music pumped through my soul as I lost myself in the movement on the dance floor that had been crudely formed by pushing all of Alfie's parent's lounge furniture against the walls out of the way. I didn't care about the room, the people or the carpet that kept trying to trip me up, though. All I could process was the music and the electric feeling it sent shooting through my veins. It was always the same. Music had this insane ability to set my soul on fire and force my body to move.

I wasn't sure Noah felt the same way, but bless him, he was humouring me. He hadn't left my side, despite me telling him over and over that he didn't have to stay with me. It was clear he wasn't a fan of dancing and I hated to think he was making himself uncomfortable on my account.

His moves were best described as 'embarrassing dad at a disco' but he was smiling and really, that was all that mattered.

We danced until I felt dizzy with thirst, and then we went in hunt of the kitchen for drinks. In the middle of the expansive kitchen floor, a raucous game of Ring of Fire had started up. I skirted round it easily, not really up for liver failure this early in the year. I'd save that for exam season.

Cocktails, though... I was here for those. I liked my

alcohol to taste like juice. None of that burning the roof of your mouth and leaving you with a sore throat nonsense.

"Lolaaaaaaaa!" A loud, drunken voice called out over the din of the game, and half a second later, a very unsteady Evie crashed into me, almost sending me flying backwards.

"Wow, pal, the party only just started. How are you so carpeted already?"

She grinned and flashed a little hip flask from her jeans pocket, like the sort my dad took to football matches in winter claiming it was 'to keep him warm'. "Had myself a little pre-party party."

"Where was our invite?" Noah asked, chuckling as he leaned over me to pour drinks for us both.

I suspected I was probably meant to feel something, the way he stood so close and allowed his body to shift against mine. But there was nothing. Nothing but a vague sense of pleasure at the attention he was paying me.

Was he flirting with me? Did he like me? And if he was and he did, why did I not feel what the other girls seemed to when an attractive guy showed an interest in them? What was wrong with me?

A cocktail would definitely help. And if it didn't, it certainly wouldn't make things worse. I didn't even know what was in the plastic cup Noah handed to me, but I downed it in just a few seconds, smacked my lips and held it out for a refill.

Noah looked at me enquiringly, shock curling his eyebrows high on his forehead. "Where's the fire?"

"I need to catch up," I muttered by way of explanation, wriggling the empty cup at him again until he took it and filled it up again.

This time, I took it a little more steady, but it wasn't long before I was on drink number five and feeling pleasantly buzzed about the whole party situation.

"Lez-dance again," I slurred, grabbing Noah's hand in one of mine and Evie's in the other, and tugging them in the direction of the flashing lights again.

Ignoring the slightly disappointed look on Noah's face, I pulled the three of us into a wonky circle and threw my hands in the air. Singing discordantly at the top of my lungs, I threw myself into the song and dragged the others along with me, until the sound of a scuffle at the bottom of the stairs ruined the moment.

"What the…?"

Rushing over along with the crowds of people, I wasn't really surprised to see Summer and Alfie standing at the bottom of the stairs, both looking dishevelled, and having a blazing row.

This was the quality content I'd come along to the party for!

His belt was undone and flapping in the air, making it very clear where they'd been and what they'd been doing. Her hair was dishevelled and her face was bright red with pure rage.

"You're trash, Alfie!" she screamed in his face. "You just float from one girl to the next and never consider anybody's feelings but your own. What the fuck is wrong with you?"

Batting her hand away as it moved to prod his chest, he smirked and replied, "Whatever. You knew what you were getting into when you went upstairs with me. Don't come at me because you thought you could change me or some shit."

"Pig!" she hollered after him as he swaggered into the kitchen and poured himself a drink, which he then proceeded to down in one go.

What was it about girls and bad boys? You saw it all the time in romance novels. The girls always seemed to fall for men who treated them like absolute garbage and everybody seemed to lap it up. I'd never been able to understand it.

Gradually, the crowd dispersed, no doubt disappointed that it hadn't kicked off more than it had, leaving Summer standing on the stairs looking genuinely crestfallen. And alone.

Hating the part of me that couldn't see a person in pain and not want to help, I shuffled towards her and we sat together on the bottom step. Head in hands, she began to cry, which made me hate my need to help even more. Nothing made me more uncomfortable than another person's tears.

"You okay?" I asked, laying my hand gently on her shoulder.

She snorted through her tears but didn't reply.

"Yeah, silly question, I suppose. Did he hurt you?"

"No," she sniffed. "Nothing like that. I just thought... Oh, never mind. I don't even know what I thought."

"You thought he'd change the habit of a lifetime and decide to commit?"

"Yes? No? I don't know. It's not like you can control who you fall for, is it?"

And here I was, out of my depth again. I had no idea what it was like to even fall for somebody, let alone the wrong sort of person. I felt like a little kid next to this girl the same age as me who had obviously gone all the way with at least one guy. Meanwhile, I still thought kissing was kinda icky and couldn't bear the thought of nudity of any kind.

In some ways, I often felt more mature than my peers, so why was I so far behind them when it came to anything to do with relationships?

"No," I whispered in response to her question, trying desperately to sound as though I knew what I was talking about. "No, I don't suppose you can."

By the end of the party, I was cheerfully drunk and absolutely determined not to get a lift home with my mum, who would definitely lecture me about the evils of underage drinking. It would have been fine, but as an accident and emergency nurse, she had all the science and horror stories to back up her points, and I really didn't want facts getting in the way of the pleasant zinging feeling in my nerves.

"You're not walking home on your own, Lola," Noah protested as I stomped my way down the driveway with determination.

"Why not? S'only about two miles. Can walk that easy," I slurred, bouncing off his shoulder and stumbling sideways until he caught me with his arm around my waist.

"Because you're drunk and it's not safe."

"Pfft," I scoffed. "I'm a strong, confident woman. Oops!" I stepped on my own point as I tripped over the curb and only avoided hitting the deck because he steadied me once again.

"Course you are," he agreed with a chuckle. "But men

are pricks and I'd never forgive myself if something happened to you on the way home."

I gazed up at him as he looked back down at me, and I grappled with confusion that fizzed around my tipsy brain maddeningly. If you were going to have a crush on a guy, Noah was the kind of guy you wanted to crush on. He was solid, dependable, sweet, funny, and even had the added bonus of being good looking. But was what I felt for him a crush, or was it just the stirrings of a newly deepening friendship? Was the faint sizzle of pleasure that coursed through me when his eyes locked so intently with mine what other girls felt when the guys they lusted after finally noticed them? And if that was the case, what in God's name was wrong with me, that when he lowered his lips towards mine, with clear intentions, I pulled away and started singing The Macarena? Except I didn't know the words so it really came out more as just one continuous sound.

He looked confused and maybe a little hurt for a moment but laughed when I danced around him in the middle of the street.

CHAPTER 6
NOAH

What was wrong with me?

I'd just tried to kiss Lola. Clearly it was the alcohol's fault because sober Noah would have never had the confidence to do that.

Despite it being the alcohol's fault, I was thankful for it because, as Lola pulled away as I moved in closer to her lipstick primed lips, the liquid poison had at least numbed the pain of rejection.

My heart sank quicker than the Heart of the Ocean in Titanic, but as I listened to her singing and watched her move her body with no rhythm or flow, my heart seemed to feel lighter than a feather.

Wasn't it strange that someone who had the power to break your heart also had the ability to fix it?

It definitely wasn't a two mile walk home. My legs ached as we trekked up and down streets that might have looked familiar if we hadn't both been drunk. We might've got slightly lost along the way, but I didn't mind. It gave me more time with Lola before I was inevitably going to have to watch her fake being sober as she walked into her house. That and the fact that I had to hold Lola up as she stumbled and swayed on and off the pavement.

But at least I had her fun and interesting conversation to keep me entertained the whole way home. I didn't think I'd laughed as hard all summer.

By the time we made it to Lola's road, I'd mostly sobered up and our conversation had turned to the secrets of the universe and why humans existed in the first place. It was the most in depth conversation I'd ever had with her, or anybody for that matter. I couldn't help but be thankful Ollie was no longer at Sandford because I knew if he'd been there, I'd have been the third wheel stumbling behind them and consumed in my own thoughts. Ollie was a good guy, but all I wanted was to be Lola's number one. Her numero uno. Just like she was mine.

"So you're saying if a meteorite was careering towards the Earth, ready to wipe out the whole of humanity, you don't think we should try to stop it?" Lola asked, incredulously.

"Nah," I answered. "Humans are the worst. Totally a failed experiment. I say let the meteor wipe us out and let the dinosaurs have another go."

"So you wouldn't even try to survive it?"

"Where would be the fun in surviving a disaster that would change the face of the Earth permanently? If there's no pizza in the post-apocalyptic world, I have no desire to live in it."

Lola laughed, her arm locked into mine as we walked

down her road. It was so easy, so comfortable with her, there was no wonder I never wanted to be away from her.

"That is fair. Pizza is the best," Lola conceded. "But I still think your survival instinct would kick in if it happened and you'd wind up at least trying."

"Well, hopefully we'll never have to find out," I replied with a deep and uncontrollable laugh.

"Oh, I don't know. If our government isn't one of the seals of the apocalypse, I don't know what will be."

My laughter grew just as she stopped in her tracks in front of a small garden. I didn't know which house was hers. I'd never walked her home before. That had always been Ollie's job.

"Well, this is me," she said, gesturing to her little terraced house. I caught her glancing over the road to what I assumed was Ollie's house. All of the houses were in darkness, which was no massive surprise considering it was almost two o'clock in the morning. "Thank you for walking me home."

"You're welcome," I said with a smile. "It's been an experience. I look forward to solving world hunger and bringing back the dinosaurs with you again soon."

"Next time, we'll discuss politics and climate change, so you best bring your A game."

"Sounds good. Sleep well, Lola-Little-Legs," I said affectionately before watching her disappear through her front door before casually walking down the street as though it wasn't two in the morning. I knew that Mum would be sitting up in bed waiting for me to get home. I knew that she wouldn't be able to settle without checking the door was locked. So with that thought, my shoes clicked a little faster against the ground.

. . .

The next morning, I woke up with a churning stomach, which seemed to grow even more unsettled the minute I tried to move, and my head thumped as I dripped with sweat. Everything ached. Even the act of blinking hurt.

Worst hangover EVER.

But it was worth it. I would have drunk everything I had the previous night ten times over to relive my time with Lola.

I knew we were friends. I often worried we'd become too close to be anything other than friends, but I was sure there was a spark between us. Lola clearly wasn't ready for a kiss and that was okay. I'd wait for her, and I hoped that my attempt at kissing her showed her I'd wait as long as I had to until she was ready to move things forward for us. If I hadn't kissed her, maybe she'd have met someone else.

The thought of Lola with another guy made my stomach heave, and the hangover wasn't helping.

If my head hadn't been spinning enough, I got to add in internalising the thought of Lola waking up in a panic that one of her friends had tried to kiss her.

You've ruined a friendship that's spanned over five years.

It's going to be so awkward being around the others.

You idiot. You've not just lost the love of your life, you've broken up a friendship group.

That morning, I did nothing but wish that Lola and I were good enough friends that we'd pull through Kiss-gate. But I also hoped that we weren't too good mates for Lola to see that I was made to be her boyfriend.

CHAPTER 7

LOLA

Somebody was drilling outside my window.

Or possibly inside my bedroom.

Or actually, feasibly inside my skull itself.

I wasn't sure, but whichever it was, it needed to stop.

My head felt like it had shrunk fifteen sizes but forgotten to shrink my brain along with it. Every inch of my cranium was on fire with pain. Nerves right across my skull and down my neck to my shoulders splintered, leaving me unable to so much as move from my bed in order to resolve the situation with pharmaceuticals.

There was a brief respite, and then the drilling started up again, this time accompanied by a wild banshee hollering my name unreasonably loud. Yanking my pillow from under my head, I pressed it over the top to drown out both the noise and the light, but they only got louder and brighter when my mum stalked into my bedroom, loudly calling my name and yanking open the curtains to let the sunlight flood in.

"Mummmmm," I groaned, even the sound of my own voice making my head rattle painfully.

"What time do you call this?" she asked, bustling around the room and not bothering to keep her voice down in the slightest.

"I don't know. Too early," I grumbled, shielding my eyes with my arm as well as the pillow.

"It's eleven o'clock. The day is half gone already. You young people always want to sleep the day away." I could hear the blatant amusement in her tone and knew for certain that she'd heard me coming in at stupid o'clock the previous night and was now passive aggressively punishing me without actually saying the words.

"I'm definitely dying," I croaked, my tongue and throat like sandpaper.

"Not until you've washed your dad's car like you promised you would, you're not."

My stomach lurched at the thought of the lively activity, and I braced myself, waiting for the vomit to follow, but I seemed to manage to stave it off by freezing in place. There wasn't going to be much chance of that if they were expecting me to wash dad's car.

"Can't it wait until tomorrow?" I rasped, wishing that in amongst all her wardrobe door slamming and tapping of her nails on my desk, she'd make a racket pouring me a glass of water and fetching half a packet of aspirin to ease the pain in my head.

"He's off to Peterborough for that business meeting tomorrow."

"Oh, fu-iddle sticks," I rapidly saved. My mum hated swearing, and the last thing I needed right now was for her to be even more mad at me than she already was.

"Mmhmm, so you better get up, hadn't you?" she barked without a shred of sympathy, and then stalked out, leaving me to my misery.

An hour and a half, and two trips to the bathroom to throw up the contents of my stomach later, I was finally upright and dressed in my comfiest, least restrictive clothes, with a bucket and sponge in my hand and a bad attitude.

The front end of the car was clean, but the rest seemed like an insurmountable mountain to climb and my roiling stomach wanted no part of it.

"They work better when they make contact with the vehicle, you know?"

I turned a scowl on Ollie as he stood there grinning at me, looking fresh as a daisy.

"You're not funny, Martin," I said without humour.

"I think you'll find I'm hilarious, actually. You're just hungover and don't have a sense of humour."

"So astute," I grumbled. "Fancy putting all that genius to work and helping a sister out? I think I'm gonna throw up again."

"What's in it for me?" He grinned and I wanted to punch him in the face.

"I'll turn the other way when I vomit?" I offered with a sickly sweet smile.

"You drive a hard bargain." He chuckled but grabbed the sponge out of the bucket and got to work.

I made the odd, cursory nod to contributing every so often, but spent most of the time shielding my eyes and trying to move as little as possible.

"Heavy night last night then?" he asked when he'd

finished and the car was sparkling in a way I never would have got it to.

"You could say that. There were cocktails and you know how I feel about alcohol that tastes like juice."

He laughed and sprayed me with the filthy water from the sponge as he chucked it back in the bucket. "Bet your mum is thrilled."

My mum was pretty cool in general. I was lucky with my parents. Especially when you considered that Ollie's dad had legged it when he'd started having a nervous breakdown and hadn't been in touch since. My parents had both stuck it out so far and for the most part they were amazing. Most of my mates thought they were strict but I didn't really see it that way most of the time. With the possible exception of today when my brain was trying to exit my skull through every possible orifice and Mum still insisted I clean Dad's car.

"Do you think I'd be out here doing this while the contents of my stomach are working their way up my gullet if she was happy?"

"Fair point. What was the occasion?"

I shrugged. "Alfie Wilson had a new conquest."

"Ooh, and how did that go?"

"Not well."

"Row on the stairs?"

"You got it. You'd think by now some of these girls would have heard something shifty about him, but they all just keep lining up like lambs to the slaughter."

"Mmm," he hummed with a smile. "His latest victim?"

"Summer Geary."

He whistled lowly. "Bet that went down well. I wouldn't want to piss her off."

"With a bit of luck, she'll cut his dick off and that'll be an end to it."

He winced, covering his crotch with his hands. "Ouch. You're a savage, Long."

"Yeah, well, let that be a lesson to you." I nodded with a small smile.

"Well, this has been fun and all, but I have somewhere to be, so…" He shoved his hand back into the bucket before pelting me with the wet sponge, sending soapy water dripping down my face.

It was not a mood improver.

"Wherever you've gotta be, it better be to the shop to buy me an emergency stash of Pepsi Max," I said with a pout, flicking some of the soap suds at him but missing by a clear mile.

"Actually, I have a date," he announced, puffing his chest out proudly like the idiot he was.

"A date…" My left eyebrow lifted sceptically and I stared him down until he relented with a sigh.

"Okay, it's a study date, but it still counts."

I laughed, swiping at the driver side wing mirror, which he'd missed and seemed to have accumulated a disgusting amount of filth since the car had last been washed. "Sure it does, princess. You keep telling yourself that. Who's the unlucky boy?"

"My English partner, Cade."

"Oooooooh." I let out a long, low whistle. "The annoying one you can't stand?"

"That's the guy."

"I better go hat shopping once I'm done here then."

"Whatever." He laughed as his eyes rolled at me, and I was pleased to see that his smile was genuine. "You missed a bit, Long." He pointed at the mirror, grinning before sauntering away, leaving me alone to the task that was so much easier now he'd done most of it for me.

By the time the car was 'Mum Clean' rather than the substantially less exquisite 'Lola Clean' I tried to get away with the first time around, my stomach had settled a little, but tiredness was trying to drag me under with every blink. All I wanted to do was fall into bed to sleep it off, but I knew Mum would never let me.

Lying about a mammoth Health and Social Care project I needed to work on, I slipped off to hide in my bedroom and grabbed my phone from its charger. If I couldn't snooze, scrolling mindlessly through TikTok for an hour would have to do instead.

I was partway through chuckling to myself at a video of a dog being paid the cheese tax when Noah's name appeared at the top of the screen. My stomach instantly began to churn, remembering the awkward way I'd blown off his attempt to kiss me the previous night. If I was being honest, I didn't even really know why I had.

> You alive, Lola-Little-Legs?

> Barely. I'm never drinking again. EVER! How about you?

> Same. Hoping even more than usual for that huge, Earth-destroying asteroid to bring forth that post-apocalyptic world we spoke about.

> What on Earth are you on about, Larson? Making my head hurt more today of all days is a bit cruel, dontcha think?

> Erm. Do you not remember? Our conversation on the way home? Do you remember anything at all from last night?

My face scrunched up as I fought to remember what we'd talked about after the attempted kiss, but all I was able to recall was the pained disappointment on his face when I'd blatantly pulled away.

> I remember... some stuff. I definitely remember your moves on the dance floor. They were... different lol.

> Yeah yeah. I know my dancing is that of legends, but what else? What stuff?

To torment him more or to put him out of his misery...? It was a fine line.

> I remember Alfie doing the robot at one point. That happened, right? Please tell me I didn't dream that because it was legendary.

> Yes, that happened. It all happened. But like, do you remember what happened after the party?!

> Which bit specifically?

It was cruel and I knew it, but bringing it up myself seemed somehow impossible. I'd have loved to pretend it never happened at all, but it didn't seem like Noah had the same plan.

> Well, obviously the talk of stopping a post-apocalyptic world from happening if you could, the slick way I slipped off the curb, and of course the promise of more world-righting chats?

My heart rate settled as I read, and I smiled at the easy, chatty tone of his message. This was the Noah I knew of old, not the guy whose lips had strayed perilously close to mine after a few drinks.

> Did anybody video the curb trip? I'm not sure I remember that!

> Well it was just me and you on the walk home, so if the footage isn't in your camera roll, unfortunately not.

> Dammit. That's disappointing. You'll have to recreate it for me sometime. :P

> Your dark and twisty wish is my command, Little-Legs. See you on Monday.

CHAPTER 8
NOAH

After a wasted, hungover Saturday and an open water swim on Sunday, Monday morning seemed to come around fast. Too quick for my liking. The butterflies that usually fluttered in my stomach at the thought of Lola had turned to dread, knowing I'd have to see her and pretend I hadn't tried to wrap my lips around hers.

I was the definition of a coward.

I could have told her; she'd given me the perfect opportunity, but I couldn't bear the thought of her not remembering and having to deal with the embarrassment and heartbreak all over again.

The walk to sixth form was just like any other as Sam and I caught up on each others' weekends. Sam's update mostly consisted of a new space game he'd debated skipping out on lessons on Friday to play. My update didn't stray from the party, only filling Sam in on the drama of that evening and not the walk home or failed kiss with Lola.

Everything was going fine until I heard Lola's voice behind me, making my stomach do somersaults.

"Isn't that right, Noah?" she questioned, throwing an arm over my shoulder, apparently deep in conversation with Evie.

"Huh? What?" I said, avoiding eye contact and maintaining all focus on putting one foot in front of the other.

"The dinosaurs are coming back for another try, aren't they? When the apocalypse comes. I'm gonna have a pet diplodocus."

"Oh, really? Don't they say people start to look like their pets after a while? You'd have to grow like... ninety feet to have a diplodocus. What about a Microraptor?" With a smug grin, I glanced up and saw Lola's bright smile and raised eyebrows.

"Are you saying I look like Dave?" she asked with a threat in her voice that I wasn't one hundred percent sure wasn't real.

"Who the hell is Dave?"

"Dave is my cocker spaniel."

"Who calls their pet Dave?"

"Mum says he's named after Dave Grohl. I say he's named after David Tennant. He says they're both named after him."

I let out a laugh and a sound that almost resembled an 'aww'. "You have a dog? I have to meet him. Especially if he talks."

"Oh my God, Dave is the best," Evie threw in, grinning at Lola and blowing her a kiss before running off to greet a friend and leaving us alone together for the first time since Friday night.

"You should definitely come round and visit him,"

Lola said after a moment of silence. "He likes it when people come especially for him. Makes him feel important."

"Oh yeah? Well, if you can check Dave's diary, I will make whatever day free to come and visit. I'd hate to make him feel unimportant."

She grinned and linked her arm through mine easily. "Dave will check his schedule and get back to you. Good weekend?"

"I look forward to hearing from him." I laughed before closing the gap between us. "Yeah, it was good. I was absolutely hanging on Saturday and went for a swim in the lake on Sunday. Really helped clear what was left of that stubborn hangover. You should come next time."

She blinked, stared at me, blinked again, then her face drew into what could only be described as a scowl. "Swimming? In the lake? You know there's a pool in town, right?"

"Yeah, but there's nothing like open water swimming. It has so many benefits, and it's free to swim in the lake."

Another blink. "You are aware that there are fish in the lake? They live there, and consequently poo there? You were literally swimming in fish shit."

Just as she finished speaking, I let out a snort, laughing in hysterics. "I'd rather swim in that than all the urine at the local pool. The fish can't help themselves, teenagers can."

"Well," she said through a laugh while her hand tapped gently against my cheek, "it's good to know you have a preference. I'll bear it in mind when I'm buying your Christmas present."

"If I receive poo or wee from you at Christmas, I think

I'll die. In fact, I draw the line at any and all gifts containing excrement."

"But you said the lake water had sooooo many benefits?" She winked playfully and my heart practically danced on the spot.

"It does, and one day I'm sure I'll get you in the lake and show you."

We walked in together through the front entrance and went our separate ways as Lola went to her health and social care class and I went to geography.

It turned out seeing Lola wasn't as hard as I'd expected, and quite frankly, I was happy pretending the kiss hadn't happened because I had my friend back.

At break time, I met up with Sam. We grabbed a quick coffee together then made our way to our IT lesson. In the corridors, I'd begun to see the aftermath of the weekend's events spilling out from the walls of Alfie's party and in through the school. Many students wore either a brightly coloured pink or blue sticker displaying either #TeamSummer or #TeamAlfie.

By the end of Wednesday, the whole school had got involved. Even pupils in year seven had stickers on despite not having been at the party. I'd spent the past few days listening to all the Chinese whispers as the facts were twisted into a dramatic tale fit for a Shakespeare play.

By Friday, Summer was spending most of her time out of lessons in floods of tears.

"Can you believe the whole Summer and Alfie thing? It's like we're living in an episode of Love Island," I said to Lola as she slurped the remains of a can of Pepsi Max.

She groaned, raking her fingers through the hair that had fallen loose from her ponytail during the day. "I wish I couldn't believe it but sadly I can. I'm sure Summer really wants all that shoving down her throat every damn day because people think it's hilarious. Last thing I'd want is my name on stickers and posters all over the place."

"Tell me about it. However, I have picked my side. I just refuse to wear one of those stupid stickers. It's not okay to humiliate someone. I mean, it's none of our business really."

"Yeah, I keep wanting to check in with her and make sure she's okay, but it kinda feels like I'm not the right person to be giving anybody relationship advice."

I looked at her, a little confused, and nudged into her. "You don't need to have a boyfriend to help someone, you know? I think Summer would appreciate a friend. I think whatever is going on is much bigger than Alfie and his ignorance."

She looked thoughtful, her brow creasing as she cast her eyes around until they fell on where Summer was walking while scrolling through her phone. "Yeah. Yeah, I think you're right. So what are you doing this weekend? Any more close encounters of the fish poo kind planned?"

"Ha, as a matter of fact, yes. My brother's taking me surfing actually. You?"

"Christ, surfing? You got some sort of death wish?" She chuckled and nudged me sideways with her elbow. "Dave will be most offended."

I ignored her death wish comment and went straight to questioning why her dog wouldn't be happy with me. "What? Wait, was I going to get a chance to meet him?"

"Well, he *was* going to invite you over for a movie night and snacks, but it seems like you have a prearranged date with death so poor Dave will have to wait."

"I'll be sure to get Dave a gift to apologise. What about the weekend after? Don't suppose Dave is free then?" I asked eagerly.

"A gift is a good idea. He likes Bonios and fresh salmon." She laughed, her hair swinging around her face as her head moved. "The following weekend could work. Obviously, he'll have to consult his busy schedule of doing nothing but sitting in the window all day screaming at passersby, but I daresay he'll make a window for you. You guys can watch Jaws. Learn about the dangers of the sea."

CHAPTER 9

LOLA

"You look so handsome!" I exclaimed, staring with complete adoration into the warmest brown eyes in existence. Straightening his bow tie and fluffing up his hair, I perfected Dave's date night appeal with a spritz of Jimmy Chow doggie fragrance just as the doorbell rang. "It's definitely going to be love at first sight."

His tail wagged adorably as he let out the cursory barks to let me know that there was somebody at the door, in spite of how obnoxiously loud the bell was.

Pulling the door open, I grinned at the sight of Noah on the doorstep, rocking back and forth on his heels with a bunch of flowers in one hand and a seriously whiffy blue plastic bag dangling from the other.

The moment Dave caught sight of his company for the evening, he launched forwards, his tail slapping against Noah's thigh as he bent instantly to fuss him. Dave wove in and out of his legs, almost knocking him right to the ground in his enthusiasm. Noah didn't seem worried. In fact, I could almost see hearts in his eyes as he mussed up Dave's ears and located the sweet spot at the top of his tail for scratches that sent him into paroxysms of delight.

"I think you have a friend for life there, pal," I said with a laugh as Noah's backside finally hit the deck with a satisfying thunk.

"I'd hope so. You're gorgeous, aren't you, Dave? Yes you are." His usual deep voice changed to the sort of lovey-dovey tone you'd use to talk to babies.

I grinned, watching the two of them with a warm feeling building in my stomach. "He dressed up especially for your date. He doesn't bring the bow tie out for just anybody."

"I should hope not. Dave looks very dapper, and you look good, too," he said, blushing a little and tugging at his collar as he battled his nerves.

I looked down at my very attractive jeans and T-shirt combo and then back up at him with a questioning look. "Umm... thanks? I worked very hard on this look, obviously."

He smiled at me, his bright blue eyes dropping to the floor. "Well, you always look nice, without even trying."

"Such a charmer," I replied with a chuckle, stepping forward to help him back to his feet before hugging him gently. "You ready to never want to go back into open water again? Jaws awaits your viewing pleasure."

"I look forward to your attempt at frightening the love of open water out of me, but I can assure you, it won't work."

I grabbed his hand and dragged him into the small living room. Mum's dark bookcases filled with romance novels made the place look smaller than it was, but she apparently *couldn't live without them.*

"Sorry, it's a bit... cosy," I said, pushing him down into the, thankfully, comfortable couch. "Can I get you a drink?"

"Water would be good. Hold the shark." Noah grinned and placed his shopping bag on the floor next to him, which Dave began sniffing eagerly.

I shuffled through to the kitchen to get his water, feeling oddly nervous without really understanding why. It wasn't like he was the first person I'd ever had over for movie night. Though, admittedly Ollie had never tried to kiss me, drunk or sober. I wasn't really his type.

The thought of Ollie reminded me that it was his not-a-crush-honest guy's birthday party that night and I could easily picture the existential crisis that was probably causing him.

As I slid back into the living room and gave Noah his water and sipped my own Pepsi Max, I glanced through the front curtains to see that Ollie's bedroom light was still on.

Rolling my eyes, I grabbed my phone and shot him a text reminding him to sort his shit out and get to the party.

> Stop overthinking and get to the party! x

I watched as the little dots appeared at the bottom of the screen telling me he was typing.

> Smart arse. I'm already there. Having a great time. :P

A small growl escaped from my chest at his blatant lie as I angry typed my reply.

> Liar. I can see your light on. Get moving.

I hate you.

> Sure you do, honey. Just like you hate the birthday boy. :P

His only reply was the middle finger emoji that made me snort and smirk in victory. Everybody knew when you resorted to emojis or swearing, you'd lost the argument.

Another text quickly followed on the heels of the last, but it wasn't Ollie this time.

Thanks for the water ;)

Cringing, I tapped the button to turn the screen dark and looked sheepishly at Noah, who was watching me with a mixture of amusement and maybe a little bit of hurt.

"I'm being rude. Sorry. I just worry about Ollie. He has a party tonight."

"That's okay. Is he okay? Glad you're back in the room, Little-Legs." He smiled and placed his phone next to him.

Frowning, I turned my dark phone over and over in my hands. Was he okay? "Some days I think he is. Then others, I just don't know," I said quietly. Ollie's story wasn't really mine to tell, but some days I felt like the worry was eating me alive.

Noah's expression softened. "All you can do is be there

for him, like you are right now. I don't know exactly what happened to Ollie, but I know how difficult coping with mental health can be. It's a daily struggle for my mum. Some days, I wish I could steal all her struggles away from her so she doesn't have to deal with them anymore."

I blinked and allowed myself to stare into his eyes for the first time. They were so blue, like the ocean on a sunny day, and they held so much sincerity that it was almost impossible to see the pain hidden underneath that he hid so well.

Reaching across to where his hand sat on the cushion beside him, I curled my fingers around his and squeezed gently. "I'm so sorry. I had no idea. About your mum. I wouldn't wish this on anybody, but hearing you say that… about taking it from them onto yourself… I feel the same so often. If I could just make him hurt a little less, maybe then I'd know he'd be okay."

"I totally get it. Thing is, you know they'd never want the same. They love us too much." Noah smiled and looked down to where our fingers had intertwined. "Mum has OCD. The real kind. Not like when people like stuff a bit organised so they say they have it. Like the kind where some days she can't leave the house because her compulsions overwhelm her so much."

My heart throbbed at the honesty mingled with pain in his tone, and my hand squeezed his once more without thought. "God, I'm sorry. That's awful. I don't know much about it but I've heard how debilitating it can be. Is she getting help?"

"There is no help. Not really. Not unless you have bucket loads of cash, which we don't. My dad works all the hours under the sun yet even that won't cut it. And Mum can't work either. She tries her hardest around the house, cooks and cleans on her good days, but on her bad days..." He shrugged sadly. "They're really bad."

Tears stung at my eyes though I fought against them angrily. I could remember all too easily the fight to get help for Ollie. Help that actually worked. The wounds on his wrists had barely healed before he was sent off on his way with a prescription and a tiny fluttering of hope in his heart that things could get better. Ultimately, though, it was his mum sacrificing everything in order to pay for his counselling that had made whatever difference had been made. He was stronger now, but sometimes he still looked so fragile to me. Maybe it was because I remembered how he'd looked in hospital with wires and tubes fighting to keep him alive, even when he'd wanted nothing more than to check out.

"I'm sorry," I whispered. "It's so wrong. People who need help shouldn't have to sell their souls to pay for it. One day, I'm going to find a way to change that."

The certainty was new, but it flooded over me like a tidal wave. Maybe *that* was the change I could bring about, the difference I could make.

"You know what, if it was anyone else saying that, I'd laugh, but not you, Little-Legs. I know you can do anything you set your mind to. I hope you know I'll be coming along for the ride and cheering you on the whole way, right?"

My cheeks coloured and my eyes locked on the spot where our hands were still joined, feeling... something... stirring in my chest—an unfamiliar something that I couldn't give a name to. All I knew was that his confidence and faith in me sent warmth flooding through me like nobody else ever had.

"You best had. I think Dave has grown attached to you already," I said, gesturing with my free hand to where Dave had curled himself up around Noah's legs with his chin resting right on his knee.

He chuckled and played gently with the fluff on top of Dave's head. The crazy pooch simply huffed a contented sigh and lifted his head into the touch. He was such a tart for affection.

"You ready to watch Jaws?" I asked after a moment of watching them with affection. "Although, by the smell of that bag you brought with you, you've got the cast of the original film in there."

"You mean this bag? Oh." Noah opened the bag, which only intensified the smell. Firstly, he pulled out a small box of Bonios, but Dave didn't seem to have the slightest bit of interest in them. His ear pricked and his tail wagged as Noah took out a piece of fresh salmon from our local butchers. "Bonios and fresh salmon, as requested. I know how to treat a dog."

I stared, first at him and then at his offerings, and my eyes began to mist unaccountably at his thoughtfulness.

"What?" he asked when I'd sat there speechless for a little longer than was strictly comfortable.

"I... just... you're kind of amazing, aren't you?"

Noah blushed and looked down with a smile. "I dunno, I just know I'd do anything for you. And Dave, of course."

Shifting a little awkwardly at his candour, I jumped up to grab the remote for the TV for something to do. "You wanna be careful saying things like that," I joked. "I could get you doing all sorts."

I stuck my tongue out at him and flopped back onto the couch beside him, before waking the TV up ready for Jaws.

As the film began with its famous two note theme tune, we settled down and wound up snuggled up together, particularly when the tense moments had me hiding my face behind cushions.

"I can't believe you voluntarily go into the water on a regular basis," I whispered when the shark killed its first victim.

"I do, but it's not like the UK is renowned for its shark infested waters. Besides, this is horror fiction. It's not real."

"First of all, how dare you? That shark is clearly real and not animatronic. Second of all, name me one film where people go into water and nothing bad happens. Pirates of the Caribbean: cursed pirates. Titanic: great big iceberg. Lord of the Flies: massive shit show. You see my point?"

Noah burst into fits of laughter before proposing the most ridiculous ultimatum I'd ever heard. "You don't give up, do you? Tell you what: if you care that much about me, how about this? I'll give up surfing if you stop drinking Pepsi Max." Noah smirked, his eyes gleaming because he knew before I'd even opened my mouth he'd outsmarted me.

"Not just a pretty face, are you, Larson? No deal. Trust me, I drink my Pepsi to keep everybody around me safe. It's a public service."

Looking smug, he replied, "Why thank you. I can't

even imagine a Lola without Pepsi Max. A shark attack would be bad, but that would be worse."

"You ain't wro-ooooh my god it's coming!" I squealed and darted behind his back as the shark claimed another victim on the screen. "Why would you do this to yourself?"

I felt Noah tense up as I shuffled behind him to hide my face. "Um, we can turn it off if you want to? I've been surfing for years now and not once have I ever bumped into a shark. Not even fake ones."

"No," I protested weakly. "I've started so I'll finish. Excuse me a moment, though. I'll refresh the drinks."

I grabbed our glasses and shuffled from the room, unable and unwilling to think too hard about why I was so disappointed that he'd tensed when I'd made contact with him.

The dinging of my text tone cut through the air once more, jerking me out of my thoughts and making me spill Pepsi Max over the kitchen counter with an aggravated sigh.

> Meet me at the park? I need you x

Panic, like ice water, frigid and merciless, seized me in its grip. Was this the bat signal I'd been waiting on tenterhooks for? Was he okay? Was he on the edge again? What would I find when I got there?

My breaths were short and gasping as I fired off a reply as quickly as I could.

> Be right there. Are you okay? x

I didn't even wait around long enough to see if he replied. Within seconds, I had my trainers and jacket on, and I crashed into the living room like a wrecking ball, unable to contain my panic.

"I'm so sorry, Noah, but I have to go. Now."

CHAPTER 10
NOAH

That day was a whirlwind of emotion—some swept me off my feet like powerful gusts as my nerves got the better of me and others picked me up and spat me out as if I'd just endured being thrown around in a tornado.

Moments ago, Lola had had her face buried into my shoulder blades as she hid from the monstrosity that was Jaws. At first, I wanted to embrace her closeness and never let her go, but her innocence dawned on me and I realised that maybe my 'date' with Lola was actually just hanging out with a friend and her dog. I tensed up in shame at the efforts I'd gone to in order to impress her.

And now, she had to leave. If she was leaving, I certainly wasn't staying.

As she fumbled with her zip in a rush and stood eyeing up the front door to leave, I jumped up off the sofa hastily. "What? What's wrong?"

She shook her head frantically, several wisps of her

poker straight black hair falling free of her messy ponytail as she did. "I don't know. It's Ollie. He needs me."

Her voice was thick with panic and there was a frenetic energy about her that had her bouncing on her toes, clearly desperate to leave.

"Okay," I said calmly, "I'm here for you. What can I do?"

"Nothing. Nothing. I just need to get to the park."

I knew the place. On occasion I'd seen Lola and Ollie hanging around on the swings as I'd walked past with friends.

"That's too far for you to walk by yourself. Especially at this time. I'll walk you there. No arguments."

Lola gave a nod, apparently not having time to argue back.

Before long, we were out the door and I trailed behind Lola, struggling to keep up as she practically ran towards the park— towards Ollie.

Damn, those little legs of hers were fast.

I didn't know what we were walking towards, but I knew for Lola to be behaving the way she was, it clearly wasn't good.

I knew the feeling all too well. The worst days were those where I had to go to school and leave Mum at home in her darkest hours, entirely unsure of what I'd be coming home to. I'd barely be able to concentrate and often the worry would be so intense I'd have to skip lunch just to go home to check on her.

Thing is, I'd have taken on all that anxiety and more if it could have saved Lola from feeling the way she did— from feeling like she had to be the one who always did the saving.

Because, aside from me, I couldn't name another person who was looking out for her.

"Slow your little legs down, Lola," I said, panting as I took huge strides to try to keep up. Her tiny feet barely touched the floor before taking another step. If she'd been a cartoon, her legs would have been drawn as circles to represent how fast she was... *walking*.

She didn't reply, instead offering me a glancing smile that didn't reach her eyes. Nothing was going to stop her from reaching Ollie, and that haunted look in her eyes told me that maybe now wasn't the best time to crack jokes.

So, I remained silent until we arrived close to the park, and stopped in my tracks when Lola came to a halt.

"You probably best not come any further. He won't want anybody else to know." She shuffled her feet slightly, her cheeks pinking in the dim light of the street lamp. "Thank you for walking me."

"Are you sure? It's pretty late."

"Yeah. Yes, I'm sure. I just need to find him. I'm so sorry about our night."

I grazed my fingers down her arm and then quickly pulled away, clearing my throat. "Don't be sorry. You've got to do what you've got to do. Maybe we could do it again sometime? I dunno."

I barely had a chance to catch my breath before her body slammed against mine and she hugged me so tight it felt like I couldn't breathe. "Definitely. Thank you. I'll text you later."

She pecked a kiss to my cheek before releasing me and taking off in the direction of the small children's play area beyond the line of trees.

My hand instinctively touched where her lips were just

seconds before as my skin tingled. My body was frozen in its place, and yet my heart pounded faster than it ever had—even faster than the rush of adrenaline that filled me when I surfed.

Was the kiss a sign of affection, something to fill me with joy until the next time I saw her, or was it a loving action from a friend? Just like the way she'd hidden behind me, using my body as a shield, protecting her from the jump scares of Jaws. Was that a friend thing? A boyfriend thing? Or a Lola thing?

The only thing that consumed my mind on that walk home was Lola, until I tried to step through the door. An overwhelming feeling of guilt consumed me as I tried the front door.

Locked. I was locked out.

But that was the least of my concerns. Mum. She did this. Her OCD would give her intrusive thoughts, awful things like worrying the house was covered in germs that would cause us all to get sick, or the fear of us being burgled. I knew that she'd have checked the door multiple times but that wouldn't have been enough to calm her. Dad would have been reassuring her on the inside.

I should be in there helping. I should have been there for her.

After ringing the doorbell a few times, I eventually heard the sliding of the bolts and locks on the other side of the door.

"Is she okay?" I said before the door was open fully, revealing Dad looking blue—his eyes red raw.

"She'll be fine. Don't worry," he said.

But I did worry. It took a lot for Dad to cry. He'd been married to Mum for nearly thirty years and had seen it all when it came to her OCD, but I'd rarely seen him cry. "Look, I'm here with Mum. Why don't you go stay at Nate's house? I'll grab you a taxi."

Before Dad could pull out his phone, I stepped through the door and shook my head. "No, Dad, I need to be here. I'll stay out of the way, but if you need anything, please come and get me?"

He ruffled my hair and smiled. "I will do. You're a good kid."

I took myself off to my bedroom, feeling on edge the whole time and listening to every slight sound. I'd have driven myself to insanity if I'd carried on, because after a while I was hearing noises that likely weren't even there.

Thankfully, the house eventually fell eerily silent as my mind continued to work on overtime, so I stuck in some earphones and listened to George Ezra.

It turned out the one thing that helped ease my worry about Mum was the person who had spent the evening worrying about Ollie. I smiled as a notification pinged in my ears, interrupting the song that was playing.

> So sorry to cut the night short. He's okay. Just needed to talk. You get home alright? x

My stomach did black flips at the kiss placed at the end of the text. First the peck on my cheek, and now this.

> I'm glad he's alright, but you never need to apologise. Yeah, I'm home. Mum's not in a good way though. I'm sat in bed feeling helpless x

It took a moment for Lola to reply, though I could see her typing and deleting over and over the entire time.

> I'm so sorry. What happened? Do you wanna talk about it? You don't have to! x

> I'll be all good, thank you. You've had enough on your plate this evening. You can take my mind off it though? I'm crying out for all the Lola Little-Legs humour right now x

> Okay, how about this...? Why do sharks swim in salt water?

> Because pepper would make them sneeze. Lol right? x

I replied with loads of laughing emojis while attempting to stop myself from laughing out loud incase I interrupted the silence of the house.

> Amazing! You really are the best. Hope it isn't long before I see you again. And Dave, of course. Hope you sleep well. Night Little-Legs x

> Nighty night, Shark Boy! Sweet dreams x

The following morning, I woke to the smell of smoked bacon and could almost hear it crackling in the pan as my mouth watered uncontrollably.

I changed my boxer shorts, slipped on a light T-shirt and pyjama bottoms, and made my way down the stairs.

Dad stood at the cooker. His eyes looked tired and his posture even more so. He didn't often make breakfast, but with the smell of Mum's favourite food filling the whole house, I knew he was doing it out of necessity.

"Is Mum alright? Are you okay?" I asked and sat down on one of the bar stools at the kitchen counter.

"We're all good. She needs some time, and to eat something," Dad said, his face not showing signs of worry but his voice led me to believe he was concerned.

"Can I go up to see her?"

"Sure you can, but don't expect too much from her. I'll be up in a second with the food. Ketchup on yours?" Dad smiled.

I nodded, plastered on a smile and walked back up the stairs and into my parents' bedroom. The room was still dark with the curtains pulled across the window, and only a bedside lamp providing a small bit of light.

"Mum? Do you need anything?" I asked, not expecting a response to avoid disappointment.

She didn't respond. She lay in bed, staring at the ceiling in her own little world. A daydream. She didn't even acknowledge that I had come into the room. She didn't see me. She didn't see anything.

I'd only seen her like this a handful of times.

Dad told me it was a way of coping, something called maladaptive daydreaming, not helped by how exhausted she must have been from the day before.

I couldn't do anything for her, and that thought made my throat fill with tears. I tried to swallow them but as dad came into the room, he placed the bacon butties straight down and wrapped his arms around me.

"It'll be okay, you know?"

I couldn't speak. I just nodded in his embrace.

I was so helplessly upset I nearly missed the cuts and

grazes on my Dad's arm, which he must have endured while supporting Mum through her intrusive thoughts last night.

There was only one thing I wanted more than Lola, and that was for my Mum to be okay.

CHAPTER 11
LOLA

Lying on my bed with my feet tapping out a rhythm on the wall and my head dangling down towards the floor, I scrolled mindlessly through my phone, waiting on a message from Ollie that never seemed to come.

I got it. He was loved up with his new crush and seemed to be spending every moment either with him or obsessing over him. But I wasn't used to spending so little time with him. We'd been each other's shadows for so long that I was struggling to remember who I was when he wasn't around. If it hadn't been for Noah's text banter, I thought I might have lost it.

Chuckling to myself, I opened up yet another article about sharks spotted off the coast of wherever it was this time and, naturally, shared it with him. It was amazing how, the moment you talked or even so much as thought about something, it would instantly fill your entire feed on every social media platform going. They were definitely reading people's minds.

> Be careful out there, shark boy. I'd hate you to lose that pretty head of yours x

You do realise there is more chance of being struck by lightning than attacked by a shark? X

> Not if you stay indoors like a sensible person. No lightning. No sharks. The worst that's gonna happen to me this weekend is paper cuts from the books I'm planning to read while you risk life and limb. x

That's before you risk your life by getting in a car to go to the book shop. BAM. Car crash. Or God forbid you decide to walk?! You'll likely be mowed down. All of these eventualities are more likely than a shark attack x

> Well, we are a ray of sunshine this morning, aren't we? Haha what's happening in the world of Noah? I'm so bored I'm actually considering studying. x

Ugh. Studying? Gross. I'm just at home x

> I know, right? Disgusting. But I'm home alone and nothing is holding my attention. I think as my resident shark boy, it's your responsibility to entertain me before I do something rash like coursework! x

Ha. Okay. Umm. Wanna do something? X

He was definitely... off. Normally, our texts were full of witty banter, sometimes bordering on the downright abusive. This weird, monosyllabic Noah bothered me and I wanted to unpick what was going on with him. He'd started to matter to me, perhaps more than I'd actually realised, because the thought of him in pain physically hurt me.

> YES! Come round. Entertain me. I have cookies! x

Be there in 15. Don't do anything I wouldn't while I'm on my way! X

Grinning, I rolled sideways off the bed, keeping still for a moment as all the blood rushed from my head after lying upside down for so long. There was a feeling in the pit of my stomach that I hadn't really experienced before. Was it excitement? It wasn't like there was anything going on between us, but his company never failed to make me smile.

Frowning at my appearance in the mirror, I made a cursory attempt at tidying my hair up before abandoning it and hoping Noah liked the dragged through a hedge backwards look.

By the time he knocked gently on the front door, I was feeling slightly manic, looking forward to his company and so ready to not be on my own.

Throwing the door open with a wide grin, I jumped forward and dragged him inside by the hand, yanking him into a hug and squeezing him while bouncing on my toes.

"I'm so glad you're here."

I felt him close his embrace tighter around me before releasing and straightening up his blue hoodie. "Wow, you really *are* happy to see me. Has boredom driven you to some sort of delirium?"

"You know, I think it might've done." I looked hard at

him, scanning him up and down and taking in his tense, tight posture and his barely there smile. Tilting my head to one side, I asked, "Everything alright with you?"

"Yeah, I'll be okay. Your hair looks… different. Good different. Did you do that for me?" He gave a small wink while wearing his best fake smile, which I could see right through.

"I probably brushed it sometime this week, yeah," I replied, frowning. "Wanna try that again?"

Noah's gaze dropped to the floor. "Just things at home are a little more intense than usual."

My heart stalled at the helpless look on his face and I couldn't help but reach for his hand once again. Pulling him through to the living room, I dropped into the couch and waited for him to copy before speaking again.

"I'm sorry. Do you want to talk about it?"

"Well. It's just." I could see him struggling to formulate words, never mind string together a proper sentence. This wasn't like him. Aside from Ollie, he was one of the only other people who could give my sarcasm a run for its money. "Mum is really struggling. She lashed out at dad a few weeks ago and since then, she's just, not herself. She's distant and dad says she's worried that she's going to hit him again. Or me."

My eyes widened as I tucked myself into the corner of the couch, facing him with my legs tucked under me.

"That sounds really hard. Has it happened before? Are you okay?"

Even though he'd said it was his dad she'd lashed out at, I couldn't help scanning his exposed skin for marks. I knew his mum was ill but I couldn't bear the thought of him hurting.

"I'm okay. I'm just worried about her. She has her bad days but its never been as bad as this. I'd do anything to take it all away, even a little. Anything to give her more of the good days." I could see his eyes swelling, fit to burst at any moment, but he didn't let them. "Anything to see her smiling more."

It hurt to swallow down the lump in my throat that formed at the desperation in his voice. The fact was, I knew exactly how he felt. That feeling of helplessness was the worst thing in the world. Watching somebody you loved more than anything at war with their own mind was its own, special sort of torture.

"Does…" I swallowed again when my voice came out hoarse. "Does she get any help?"

"What help? She goes to the doctors but I don't actually think there's much they can do. Maybe if we won the lottery things would be different."

An old, familiar anger burned in my stomach at his words. Words I was all too familiar with. Only the people who could afford it could get the help they needed.

"Yeah," I whispered. "Yeah, I get that. The entire system is so wrong. It shouldn't matter what you have in the bank. If people need help, they should be able to get it." I knew my voice was slowly rising in volume and that I was probably making it really awkward, but my anger at Noah's situation, at Ollie's, was a fire burning me up from the inside.

"Tell me about it. I mean, I guess I'm lucky I don't get too involved with Mum's doctor's appointments and medication and stuff, but I've seen how frustrated Dad gets." Noah drew patterns in the carpet with his feet, still maintaining eye contact with everything other than me.

"That must be really hard?" I asked quietly, reaching my arm along the back of the couch, not quite around his shoulders but almost.

"It is. But I know I'm not alone. I have my Dad and my brother… and you."

I smiled genuinely for the first time since I'd seen his sad face on the doorstep and nudged his shoulder lightly. "Too right you have me. I've claimed you as my own now. You're stuck with me."

"That really does make me happy. Thank you." He finally looked up at me and studied my smile for a while before returning one. "Are you going to offer me a brew? I'm parched."

I laughed and felt something inside me relax at the sight of his usual, genuine smile. "One brew coming right up. With cookies. Because sugar makes everything better, right?"

"Soooooo," Evie sang as she slid into the seat next to me in health and social care the following Wednesday.

"So?" I took a long drink of Pepsi Max, curling my eyebrows at her over the can.

Grinning, she nudged me with her shoulder playfully. "What's going on with you and Noah Larson?"

Slamming the can down on the table, I spun around to fully face her in surprise. "What do you mean?"

"Oh come on! There's no way you haven't noticed the way he looks at you."

I stared at her while an unpleasant feeling began to stir in my stomach.

"We're friends. That's all."

"Uh huh. Sure. Friends look at you like that all the time. One hundred percent."

"He doesn't look at me any different to anybody else," I protested weakly, scanning back through my memories and conveniently ignoring the ones that made her words ring with truth.

"Oh, honey," she crooned patronisingly. "You really haven't noticed? That boy has it bad."

Frowning at her, I fiddled awkwardly with the ring pull on my now empty can. "But that's…"

"Accurate?"

"Crazy," I corrected, ignoring the voice in my head that was trying to remind me that he'd tried to kiss me at the party.

Her head tilted sideways and she ignored Mrs Leary's call to order completely in favour of carrying on the conversation. "What's crazy about it?"

"Well, he's…" My arms flailed wildly around my head as I battled to find words to explain the complete impossibility of the phenomenon she was pushing. "He's Noah, isn't he? All blond haired, blue eyed surfer boy. And I'm…"

What?

Not even sure I'm into him?

Not even sure I'm into any boy?

Not even sure I'm a proper person?

"I'm just me," I finished lamely. "Just Lola."

"Oh please," she said, tossing her thick black hair over her shoulder. "You're a total catch. If I weren't tragically straight, I'd totally want you."

"Tragically straight?" I asked through a chuckle.

"Have you seen the boys in this place? The only decent one in the place is obsessed with you." Her voice was half mocking, half serious, and when Mrs Leary finally managed to call the class to order, I was left feeling more lost and confused than ever.

If she was right, which I suspected she was, and Noah did feel more than just friendship between us, how did I feel about it?

I liked him, sure. What was not to like? Sure, he'd tried to kiss me that one time, but we'd both been really drunk and neither of us had mentioned it since.

I loved hanging around with him. He had the best sense of humour and always made me laugh. Not to mention how sweet and kind he was.

He was every girl's dream, right? The perfect surfer dude dreamboat. So there was absolutely no way I could *not* want to be with him.

Was this non-committal *maybe* feeling the sentiment that other girls got all giggly and googly eyed over?

Sure, being around Noah made me feel warm inside, but I'd always assumed that I'd want more than just to hang out with the boy I eventually fell for.

When the girls in my classes talked about the lads they were with or fancied, they seemed to want so much more.

So what was wrong with me?

If I couldn't get giggly over Noah Larson of all people then maybe I really was broken.

Maybe a part of me was missing—the part that went weak at the knees at the sight of topless superheroes and wanted to cake my face in makeup on the off chance that a boy would want to stick his tongue down my throat. Which, by the way, was totally gross!

CHAPTER 12

NOAH

was in love with Lola Long. Madly in love. It was killing me.

So I decided to do what any normal, rational teenager would do in my situation.

I ran.

I packed my weekend bag, hopped onto my brother's camper, and off we went—a weekend away at the beach to do nothing but ride the surf. I couldn't wait for the sea wind to batter against my face to help filter out all the thoughts of Lola. I was desperate for the sea water to wash away some of the worry that was pent up inside for Mum as well as the constant ache of knowing I was helpless to do anything about what she was going through.

We left as soon as Nate had finished whatever dull after school revision club he held on a Friday and spent the next few hours on the motorway watching the flickering of brake lights illuminating the evening sky.

I had to listen to my brother's eardrum rupturing singing to songs he claimed were cool back in his day. You wouldn't normally have believed there was nearly a decade between us—his lack of maturity made sure of that. But the minute a radio station played just one song he considered new, he'd switch it over immediately to a station playing songs from the eighties. He hadn't even been born then, yet he claimed the music to be his era.

There's no wonder why he's still single. He really doesn't help himself.

We arrived at our favourite spot late into the evening. The sun had already set and the moon made the sea glisten under its warm, white glow. It was a pity we had to wait until the following day to get on our boards. I would have called it a night there and then if I hadn't been so hungry and Nate hadn't already set out to grab us our evening meal from a local fish and chip shop. I would have settled for some fast food on the way but Nate didn't believe in service stations. 'Overpriced and no quality', that's what he'd say. And that was just his view on the food inside, I wouldn't even dare start a conversation about the 'daylight robbery' of fuel prices at service stations.

I found myself alone in the campervan, and it turned out that the thoughts of Lola I'd tried to run away from had also packed an overnight bag and come along for the ride. I couldn't get her out of my head.

I'd barely seen her for a couple of weeks since I'd confided in her about Mum, occasionally bumping into her in the corridors, which was hard enough. It felt like she was avoiding me, which only made my stomach turn and my heart ache.

I did know that she'd been invited to some fancy

bonfire night party by Ollie. I'd have been lying if I'd said I didn't want to be at the party with her.

Images filled my mind of Lola dancing, the reflection in her eyes glowing at the demand of the bonfire. I smiled through the deep sadness I felt and pulled out my phone to text her.

> Hey Lola-Little-Legs. You alright? Hope you have a good night at the bonfire party tomorrow. I'm away for the weekend, but if you need me, I'm here x

I stared at my phone waiting for a message in return, but it didn't come. The sound of Nate pulling open the camper door made me jump and lock my phone instantaneously.

"Bro, get a load of this fish," he said, unwrapping the chip shop paper and unveiling the biggest battered cod I'd ever seen. I swallowed hard and wiped my lips to stop me from drooling, quite pleased we hadn't stopped at a service station after all.

"Wow. This looks great. Thanks, Nate. I really do like our trips away." I smiled while grabbing a handful of fresh chips, the heat burning my hand for seconds after throwing them on my plate.

"Don't mention it. It's good for me, too," he said, exhaling a few times to cool the chips he'd already shovelled into his mouth.

We sat next to each other with our plates on our laps, too busy eating to talk, until my phone buzzed and lit up at a text from Lola.

> Hey, where have you gone? Shark baiting again? Send pics of your injuries!

I grinned at her response and quickly typed out a reply.

> You know it. If I'm sending pictures of my injuries, I expect pictures of the countless drinks you'll be downing tomorrow!

I looked up from my phone to Nate and waited for the usual teasing to commence about having a girlfriend, but it didn't come. He simply smiled.

Oh god. What's wrong with him? Is he dying?

"So, is it the usual plan for tomorrow?" I tried to make conversation. Clearly I needed to determine if my real, immature brother had been abducted.

"Yeah. Absolutely," he said, still chewing his food. "We'll wake up, grab an early breakfast then hit the waves. The forecast is looking good for the boards tomorrow, but the sea is gonna be chilly."

What was with him? He'd gone all serious. I wondered if he'd been bollocked by the head teacher for his incessant childish behaviour. I had to stop myself from smirking at the thought of my grown up brother being told off.

Clearly, I had my work cut out with him. "Cool. Sorry about the text, by the way. I know we like to come here and escape. It was Lola."

"Oh yeah? How is she?" he said casually.

I looked at him blankly. "Umm. She's fine, I guess."

He took another large bite of his fish and spoke with a mouthful. "Good. You know, maybe one time she could come away on a weekend break with us, if you wanted?"

"Ha. Thanks for the offer but I think coming on a surfing holiday with us would be Lola's worst nightmare." I snickered at the thought of her watching me surf offshore, holding up a Jaws poster and scattering flowers on the beach. "Besides, I quite like it being just the two of us."

"Oh. Yeah." Nate cleared his throat. "Me, too."

After watching a couple of episodes of The Inbetweeners, we pulled out the bed and got into it next to each other, topping and tailing, as usual. I had to admit, despite my brother acting so oddly, rather than his usual antics where he could have literally been a character in The Inbetweeners, my head seemed clearer and I hadn't even been out on the waves yet.

I rested my head on the pillow, trying to ignore the bright glow of my brother's phone lighting up half of the camper van and his fingers tapping against the screen. Had he forgotten we had a whole day of surfing planned? I needed to sleep. I looked up to see his smile, as bright as the screen, completely in his own little world. One mighty kick under the covers pulled him right out of whatever new happy place he'd found.

"Ouch. Bro. What was that for?" His hand slipped under the duvet to rub right where my foot had met his ribs.

"It was weird seeing you smile that much. It grossed me out. Be moody or sarcastic like everybody else."

Nate snickered and placed his phone down. "How can I when you're currently pouting enough for the both of us?" He spoke in his baby voice and lunged himself over to my side of the bed, rubbing his knuckles against my head. "Is that better, Noey?"

"Ahhhhhhh," I screamed loudly, likely alerting the rest of the campsite as I managed to escape the headlock my brother had put me in. I quickly grabbed his phone and jumped up, stepping on his chest. "Cease fire, or I'll text Dad and tell him it was you that scratched his car, not the window cleaner."

"You wouldn't." Nate pulls my leg, forcing me to lose my balance and land on the bed, the very thin mattress breaking my fall.

"I would." I clicked the side button, lighting up his locked phone. An unread text message sat on the front screen as a notification.

> You can't tell him about us. Not yet xx

Nate sat up and moved the cover out of the way, knowing full well I was likely looking at a message from Emma.

"Why can't you tell me about you and Emma?" I asked.

Nate's hands met his face with a sigh. "Look. I wanted to tell you. I really did. I didn't want you to find out this way, but you have to *swear* you won't say anything." Nate looked me dead in the face. This was why he had gone all serious. He'd met a bloody woman.

"Ugh. Fine. I won't tell anyone about your secret girlfriend. Why are you bothered if people know?"

"I met her at school…" Nate said.

I cut him off before he could say another word. "She's a student? No way!"

"No. Of course she's not a student. What do you take me for, Noah?" The pitch of his voice was at an all time high. "She's a teacher. We don't want the pupils finding out about us. Not yet, anyway. It's really new for us. You cannot say a word. Not even to your girlfriend, Lola."

"She's not my girlfriend." I glared at him and then laughed. "I've got to say, I'm a little relieved it's not a student. So, tell me about this Emma of yours?"

"There's nothing to tell yet. She's hot. Smoking even. She teaches English and has this incredible way with words. Like, no matter how hard I try, I can't keep up with her or win any arguments, which I kind of like. And, well, that's all you really need to know for now. Maybe when we've been together a little longer, she could come on a weekend trip with us?" Nate smiled, and although I was sad that this could be our last trip just us two for a while, and that he was growing up (finally), how could I say no? A no would be like a sucker punch to his stomach, when the only reason I got to do what I loved was because of him.

"You want me to go on holiday with someone who passed their teaching qualification by their liberal use of Google, and with an actual teacher?" I smirked despite receiving a wallop from Nate. "I guess I can do that."

"Thanks, Noey." Our hands met in a brotherly handshake and we tucked ourselves back into bed.

I was just drifting off when I heard Nate speak. "You aren't going to tell Dad it was me, are you?"

"Night, Nathaniel," I replied.

CHAPTER 13
LOLA

Noah was away, engaging in those god-awful extreme sports of his, and as much as I hated to admit it to myself, I missed him. He'd texted once, but it was pretty clear he was busy in the water and spending time with his brother.

I must have typed out and deleted a hundred messages since he'd been gone, sharing random mundane stuff that probably wasn't all that interesting but somehow made me think of him.

And now, standing once again in front of my wardrobe having an existential crisis about my clothing choices, I found myself once again reaching for my phone and typing a message before I'd even thought about it.

> What does one even wear to a Bonfire Eleganza anyway?

My thumb hovered over the send button for a really long time before I sighed and deleted it. Noah surely wouldn't care about the wardrobe malfunction that was my life, and Ollie would be too busy angsting over looking good for the boy he *'definitely wasn't in love with'*.

In the end, I settled on a black, lace skater dress that made me feel just the right amount of girly without being ridiculous. I prevaricated with some makeup and then had a look at the finished product in the mirror with a sigh. I'd never be one of those girls who looked elegant and effortlessly beautiful, but I figured I'd do. Tonight was all about Ollie anyway. He was head over heels for a guy in his English class despite his protests to the contrary, and I wanted nothing in the world more than for him to be happy.

I couldn't conceive of a time when I wouldn't worry constantly about him, but maybe, just maybe, if I knew he was more settled, I'd be able to switch it off from time to time.

When we met on the street outside our homes, I twirled for him and then he did the same for me, holding his jacket open as he spun, his eyes desperately seeking approval for his black suit, white shirt and skinny black tie.

"You'll be the most handsome guy there," I said with a smile, and pecked a kiss on his cheek.

He didn't comment on my appearance, but I hoped it was because he was distracted and not because he thought I looked like a swamp demon.

A long, low whistle erupted out of me when I caught sight of Cade's enormous house. It looked big enough to hold at least five of the houses on our street and still have room for stables and a five car garage.

"Jeez, Ols, you didn't tell me that you had a crush on Mr freaking Darcy."

"I do not have a cr–" he instantly began to protest, but gave up when he saw the sceptical look on my face and dropped into a put-out silence.

"So tell me, buddy, did you fall for him before or after you found out he was loaded?"

"It's just a house, Lols," he muttered, not taking his eyes from the gate at the side of the house nervously.

"Not in the mood for jokes. Gotcha," I mumbled back, linking my arm through his and nudging his hip with mine. "You ready?"

He inhaled deeply several times before nodding and allowing me to sweep him along into the vast garden at the back of the house. We both gasped at the sight in front of us. Eleganza was right. Evidently, Cade knew how to stage a party. Everything was perfect, like something out of an unrealistic American rom-com. Fairy lights twinkled around us, and crystal glasses filled with what looked like Champagne flashed in the flickering light of the giant bonfire that took centre stage.

We both took a glass as a tray danced past on the hand of a waiter clad all in black, and I tapped my glass against Ollie's with a smile. He looked like he was going to be sick.

"Relax. It's only a panic attack if it comes from the right region of France. Otherwise, it's just sparkling anxiety."

His lips curled at my terrible attempt at a joke, and he took a long drink, presumably seeking more courage than he was currently in possession of.

Squeezing his arm, I knew the exact moment he clapped eyes on his Mr Darcy. His entire body went taut and his eyes locked on a single figure who looked dressed for a catwalk. I had to hand it to Ollie; the guy was dreamy. I couldn't blame him for falling for the guy. And he was *wearing* his fancy outfit, a fact that clearly hadn't bypassed Ollie, who seemed to be suddenly mute beside me.

I watched with interest as Cade didn't hesitate, even for a moment, before going in for the hug. They exchanged short greetings, but I didn't tune into their words, too interested in watching the way they seemed to automatically fit together, like they were puzzle pieces that had been missing one another all along.

And then I heard my name, and my attention snapped away from their body language and back to the conversation at hand.

"And you must be the famous Lola," Cade said, turning that charming smile of his onto me, beaming brightly. "Thanks so much for coming. This one is a bit flighty without his Emotional Support Human."

I grinned, flipping my hair much more confidently than I felt, and tucked my arm through Ollie's, dragging him into my side.

"Oh, wild horses wouldn't have kept him away from tonight," I said playfully. "It's all he's talked about, isn't it, Ols?"

He swatted at my arm, a little harder than I thought was necessary, but his face was amused when he replied, "Thanks, Lolz. I can always count on you to humiliate me."

I was certain Ollie hadn't noticed, but Cade's eyes had lit up at my words, and there was no denying the pleased expression that creased his face into a beaming smile.

I couldn't help smiling right on back. So far, I approved

of him. "You're welcome, buddy," I replied with a grin. "Got your back."

Cade's eyes glittered with good humour, and he smiled at Ollie so warmly that it seemed to actually heat the air around us by several degrees.

"I can see why you two get on," he said cheerfully to Ollie before turning that megawatt smile onto me. "I think we're gonna get on, too."

Yeah, I liked him. He stood a chance of me allowing him to be Ollie's one and only without risking me braining him. Grinning, I stepped up beside him and linked my arm with his.

"Oh, Cade, you and I have so much to catch up on." There were so many stories I could tell him, so many ways I could embarrass Ollie. But the most pressing thing of all was ensuring that Cade understood just how important Ollie was and how lucky he was to have caught his eye.

We made our way to the bar together with the sounds of Ollie's protests ringing out behind us. I tormented him like a best friend absolutely should, fake whispering in Cade's ear the whole way while all I actually said to him were a few simple words.

"He's precious. Take care of him."

That warm smile of his heated even further as he took my hands in his and said, with utter conviction, "I promise I will. I already know how special he is."

At his words, something inside me settled. Something I hadn't even known was there. A nagging doubt borne of worry for the friend I'd come so close to losing. A what if... deep inside. What if Cade wasn't the right guy for Ollie? What if Ollie was on a one-way track to getting his heart broken? What if Cade was just another person intent on making Ollie's life even more miserable?

But there was no lie in his words. Every single one was filled with conviction and truth.

It made me laugh when Ollie finally caught us up and forced himself between us with an indignant expression and a sassy hand on one hip. "Do you guys want to be alone, or…?"

Cade's reply of, "Actually, yeah. Give us twenty minutes," had me sputtering out a laugh while Ollie looked even more put out.

He didn't have chance to reply, though, before a whirlwind of blonde hair cut through the gathering with a screech of, "Bestieeeee. Oh, and you." She paused, pointing to Ollie and poking him with every word. "I've not seen you two together since you were getting cosy in Cade's dance studio."

I smiled and laughed along with everybody for a couple of seconds more until my brain translated what blondie had just said into Lola language.

"Wait," I hollered, torn between shock and hurt at the fact I was finding out about this through a stranger. "You were doing what in his where?"

I blinked at Ollie who did at least have the decency to look sheepish, but before anybody had the chance to reply, blondie had swept two drinks off the bar and thrown one arm around my shoulder as though we'd known each other all our lives.

"Do I have so much to tell you?" she practically sang in my ear. "Let's not cramp these guys' style."

And we were off, her strong arm leading me through

the party—who were all these people anyway?—and into Cade's cavernous house.

I paused instantly, taken aback at the sheer size of the kitchen the huge French doors opened up onto. My mouth fell open and I literally gawped like a goldfish, while her arm attempted to urge me on.

"I know," she said in a slightly bored tone. "Cade's house is ridiculous. You get used to it after a while. If you follow me, I know where the good snacks are hidden for later on. He always keeps some back."

Giggling conspiratorially, she led me through into another room.

"*Two* kitchens. There are two kitchens in this house. Who even needs two?"

Blondie's eyes rolled so violently I was worried she'd rupture something.

"I know, right? Especially two people who I don't think have ever cooked in their lives before."

"You're right. Ridiculous is absolutely the word for this place. Ollie never told me he was crushing on Rockefeller."

"But," blondie went on with a grin wider than the enormous house, "If you just follow me through here... Yes! Voila. The good snacks."

She'd dragged me by the hand through a door that was invisible from the entryway to the second kitchen, into what looked like a utility room with extra storage. Covering the counters were plates and plates filled with food, plus bags and bags of packets of extras, ready to go later in the party.

"I *knew* there would be pizza!" Blondie exclaimed, rushing forward and instantly peeling the cellophane off a huge tray of mini pizzas, and stuffing at least three in her mouth at once.

"Umm..." I hesitated, standing in the doorway watching her as she grabbed two bags full of God knew what and made herself comfortable sitting on a spare bit of counter. "Not to be rude, but... Who actually are you?"

"Oh my God," she spluttered through a mouthful of pizza. She held up a single finger, keeping eye contact with me as she chewed at double speed until the pizza was all gone. "I'm sooooo sorry. You must think I'm a psycho. I just got so excited that the other best friend is here that I got carried away. I'm Hannah, Cade's bestie. And you're Lola, right? Otherwise, this is awkward as hell."

Privately, I thought it was pretty awkward even with her having got the right person, but I kept quiet about that. "How do you...?"

"Had to listen to Cade mooning over whether or not you were Ollie's girlfriend, didn't I? Honestly, that boy's gaydar is all over the place."

"But yours is...fully functional?"

"Oh God yes. Pride myself on it. As what seems like the only lesbian in this godforsaken town, I have to keep it sharp in case the love of my life shows up and I'm not ready."

I stared at her for a long moment, allowing the silence to eat up the space between us as I wondered what she saw when she looked at me. What must it be like to be so sure of your own identity that nothing and nobody could make you doubt it?

Me? I didn't know what I felt, or what I even wanted. There was a part of me that wanted to like Noah back as much as he allegedly liked me. There was no doubt that I loved being around him, but the thought of... more with him? More with anyone? I just wasn't sure.

"You okay with that?" Hannah asked when the silence had dragged on for a little too long. "The lesbian thing, I mean. I know some people are-"

"Dicks?" I interrupted, earning a snort of laughter from her.

"I knew I was gonna like you, Lola." She reached her hand out to me, beckoning me to sit beside her on the counter. I hopped up and shifted back against the wall, bringing my knees up to my chest, accepting a mini pizza from Hannah with a grateful smile.

I nibbled around the edges, my eyes focused tightly on the small snack, trying to work up both the nerve and the words to ask Hannah what I wanted, perhaps even needed, to know.

"H-how did you know?" I asked eventually, my fingers tangling together awkwardly around my knees, fidgeting with the lace of my dress. "That it was girls you liked. Like... did you just *know* or did you have some sort of lightbulb moment?"

She considered me for a moment, her head tilted to one side, her expression thoughtful. Maybe she was trying to work me out. I knew I was.

"Well, I always knew I wasn't into boys like the other girls. Once the hormones kicked in, they used to get all giggly whenever the popular lads would so much as sneeze in their direction, and I could never understand what all the fuss was about. And then in year eight, I had this teacher for science. Miss Locke, she was called. God, she was the most beautiful thing I'd ever seen in my life. All of a sudden, I felt like I got it. I would've done anything for her. Even just to get her to smile at me." Her expression had turned dreamy and her voice had softened to a low, affectionate tone. "Overnight, I went from being disdainful of all those girls doing their hair a certain way, rolling their skirts up, or vaping just to impress the boys, to doing everything I could to get Miss Locke's attention. Before her, I hated science. Half the time I used to try to skip it, but once she was my teacher, I suddenly couldn't get enough of chemistry. Stupid, right?"

I shrugged. "I dunno." And I didn't. I really didn't. I'd never experienced that–that need to be around somebody constantly, to try to attract their attention, to change elements of myself to make myself more attractive to somebody else. It was foreign to me. Did that mean there was something wrong with me? Did I have some fundamental part missing?

"Hey," Hannah said, her voice suddenly soft and thoughtful. "Where did you go?" Her hand landed gently on mine where it was tangling roughly with the material of my dress.

"Sorry," I replied quietly, feeling lost, a wobble in my voice. Would I ever figure out where I belonged? Then, mortified, I swiped at a single tear that had found its way clear of my eyes and was weaving its way down my cheek.

"You don't have to be sorry," she said kindly, squeezing gently at the hand still curled into the fabric. "I know we only just met and all, but I'm a really good listener if you need to talk. Or I can get Ollie for you if you'd prefer?"

"No!" I instantly croaked. I didn't want to bother him

with this right now. Not when I didn't even know what was going on with me.

"Did I say something wrong?"

"No. No, it's not you. I just… I guess I wish I could be so sure of… anything."

"What do you mean?"

"Well, you guys, you just seem so sure of who you are, what you want, and I'm here like…" I didn't know how to put my feelings into words. The best I could do was a shrug that encapsulated all my fears and confusion in one simple gesture.

"Oh, honey, you think because I know the chromosome configuration of the people I want to be with, that means I know who I am? Being a lesbian doesn't define me as a person, no matter how much Cade tries to convince me that it does. You aren't only the people you choose to be with. You're so much more than that. You can spend a lifetime building your identity and still not be comfortable and safe in a definition of who you are as a person. Most people grapple with that until the day they die. Who you sleep with might be a part of your identity but it's not the be all and end all."

"Wow," I breathed. "You sound so… wise. You sure you're our age?"

She laughed, nudging her body up right next to mine and throwing an arm over my shoulder, squeezing in a reassuring way that sent warmth flooding through me. "I have much wisdom, young padawan. But you seem confused. Can I help?"

My head dipped on my shoulders and I stared at my twisting hands. "I just don't feel like I fit anywhere, you know?"

"In what way?"

"In every way, really. Like you said, all the girls at college are obsessed with lads. It seems like their entire lives revolve around impressing their latest crush or whatever. And I'm just here like… meh."

Her thumb moves in soothing circles on my arm as I allow my head to fall onto her shoulder as though we've been mates forever.

"Not a fan of the fellas?"

I shrug again. "I don't know. They're okay, I guess. They just don't drive me wild with hormones or whatever. But then, neither do girls. I thought for a bit I might be a lesbian. I sort of wish I was to be honest. At least then I'd know. But I don't really wanna do all that… stuff with girls anymore than I do with guys. If I'm being honest, I find it all a bit icky."

"Icky," she repeated, her tone a mixture of amusement and curiosity.

"Icky." I nodded. "All those body fluids swapping all over the place. Other people's body parts inside yours? Icky."

She went quiet for a moment, and when I twisted to look at her, her expression was thoughtful rather than mocking like I'd expected it to be.

"Have you considered the possibility that you might be ace?" she asked cautiously after what felt like forever.

I blinked and stared at her in confusion. "I mean, that's very kind and all but I'm not sure it's relevant?"

Hannah laughed again, a whole body laugh this time. "No, honey. I mean ace as in asexual. It kinda sounds like you might be."

My face scrunched up at her words and I hadn't even

had time to think or formulate a response before my mouth shot one off anyway. "What, like a fungus?"

Another laugh.

"Not quite. An asexual as in somebody who doesn't experience sexual attraction the way non-aces do. That's all. Sound familiar at all?"

I hummed non-committally.

Asexual.

It was a word I'd only ever come across in science lessons before, usually relating to fungi or amoebas or something. I wasn't sure what to make of Hannah sitting there using it to refer to humans. To *me*.

"I don't... Is that even a thing?"

She offered me an indulgent smile. "What do you think the A stands for in LGBTQIA plus?"

"Uh... I never really thought about it, I guess."

"Perhaps it's time that you did. Look into it, see what you think. Sexuality and identity isn't a one size fits all. I'm sure no two aces are the same, the same way that no two lesbians or gays are the same, but it might help you to find out more. Do a little digging."

"But.. I... What would it mean? For me?" *For Noah*, I added silently.

"It means," Hannah started, squeezing me even more tightly than before, "that, just like everybody else, you make choices about what you want from your life and from your relationships. Some aces have partners, and some don't. Some have sexual relationships, and some don't. You get to make those choices. Nobody else can make them for you."

My mind churned, Hannah's words getting lost and muddled in a tornado of information and emotions.

No matter what Hannah said, being asexual sounded, to me, a lot like dying alone surrounded by cats.

"I better go," I said suddenly, uncurling myself from her and jumping down from the counter, unable to meet her eyes. "Ollie is probably wondering where I've got to."

"Sure," Hannah replied hesitantly. "And hey, if you need to talk…" She produced a pen, apparently from nowhere, and grabbed my hand before I could scarper.

When she released it, eleven digits were written neatly on the back of my hand with a tiny love heart underneath.

"Call me, text me, send out a carrier pigeon. Whatever you need. You don't have to figure this out all alone, okay?"

"Yeah… Yeah, thanks," I muttered, not taking my eyes off the phone number as I took off through the gigantic house and back into the garden in search of Ollie.

I hadn't made it far before a hand caught hold of mine, and I turned to see Hannah looking at me with concern.

"Hey, are you okay? I didn't mean to freak you out."

"You didn't," I forced out. "It's just… a lot to think about. That's all."

"I know," she agreed softly. "But… use the number if you need to. Or even if you don't. Who doesn't need more mates in their life, right? We could get coffee, chat about those pesky boys of ours and their love lives."

The love lives of people who had them were the last thing I wanted to deal with in that moment, but I offered a smile anyway and hoped it looked more amused than freaked out.

Then a voice I knew all too well cut through my thoughts.

"It really was a great party. You're amazing."

Ollie and Cade were standing looking sickeningly coupley together, which made my stomach churn with a mixture of jealousy and anxiety over my own future.

"Oh, God, steady on," Hannah called out with a laugh. "You'll make his head even bigger than it already is."

We exchanged pleasantries or something similar that I waded through with a mind that felt like it was full of treacle, then Ollie and I left together, his arm looped through mine. I could feel him practically buzzing out of his skin, but all I wanted was to be alone. To think. To figure things out. Quite possibly to cry where nobody could see me.

"I have got *so* much to tell you," he said eventually, bouncing like a damn tigger.

"Oh?" I grunted, attempting to sound interested when his successfully blossoming love life was the last thing I wanted to hear about.

"We kissed," he announced joyfully, clearly expecting me to share his excitement.

"That's cool," I replied dully, unable to raise even the slightest smidge of enthusiasm.

"Cool? Really?"

"Yeah, Ollie. Cool. I'm happy for you. What do you want me to say?"

I wasn't being fair. This was a huge moment for him and even as I spoke, I hated myself, but I couldn't stop hearing Hannah's words reverberating inside my head.

Some aces have partners, and some don't. Some have sexual relationships, and some don't.

"I don't know," he replied, clearly stung. "I guess I was expecting a little more than cool."

"Well, I don't know what to tell you, buddy. Maybe,

just maybe, the whole world doesn't revolve solely around you."

I could see my house now, and before Ollie could say anything, I took off running. I could feel tears stinging at my eyelids, threatening to rain down my cheeks, and I needed to be on the other side of the front door before I'd allow them to fall.

When it slammed home behind me, I dragged in a deep but ragged breath, my back sliding down the wood until I hit the floor and the tsunami of tears flowed free, accompanied by body-shaking sobs of confusion, fear, envy, and a million other emotions I couldn't have given a name to if I'd tried.

CHAPTER 14
NOAH

"What happened to you? I better be the first to sign that," Sam said, strolling out of his house a whole five minutes late.

"So it's noticeable then?" I laughed and pulled a permanent marker from my coat pocket, which I knew I'd inevitably need for everyone wanting to sign my cast. Sam ordered me to keep still and wrote his name in a funky block pattern, before heading to Sandford.

I hadn't expected to come home with a broken arm. Lola was never going to let me live this down. She was going to be insufferable. Even so, I was looking forward to seeing her.

I'd not heard a peep from her the whole weekend, which either meant Ollie wasn't okay or she was mortally hungover, and for Lola's sake, I hoped it was the latter.

I didn't bump into her at the gates like normal and escaped her incessant badgering about my injury because I arrived late. I went straight to my first lesson, geography, and had the joys of a hyperactive Alfie to brighten up all our Monday mornings.

"Yo, Miss, are you sure you don't wanna come to my party?" he yelled from the back, swinging on the hind legs of his chair.

"Another party, Alfie? Whatever for this time?" Miss Hunt teased while moving to the next slide on urbanisation.

"Because it's nearly Christmas. Just a casual one. It'll be fun. Everyone loves a party."

"Ahh. For a second I'd hoped your party was going to be in direct relation to geography, so as much as I'd love for everyone to discuss your *casual Christmas party* in more detail, we have work to do and your mock exams are looming." Laughter erupted in the classroom but after a stern look, the room fell into silence and we began to learn more about the delights of human geography. It was the worst kind of geography in my eyes, but if I was going to pass my exams, I knew I had to focus.

The lesson came to a close and Alfie placed his arm on my shoulder as we walked down the corridor.

"You're invited to my party by the way. After last time, I'm trying out a different kind of party. This time, I'm not having a house full, just a few people I think are pretty cool. You're one of them," Alfie said and I nodded along, smiling. Alfie and I weren't close, but I appreciated the compliment. If we'd had royals, he would have been the king of Sandford Sixth Form, and I certainly wasn't going to piss off the king.

"Cheers, Alfie. I'll be there. Is Lola invited?"

"I haven't invited her yet but sure, she can come. You

can invite her for me if you like?" Alfie said with a smile and a wink.

"Okay, I will. Wanna sign my cast?" I pulled out a pen and we stopped in our tracks, forcing other students to walk around us while Alfie wrote his name and then drew the obligatory penis and balls next to the name of one of his friends.

I didn't end up seeing Lola until lunch time. She walked around the corner with a shopping bag, linked arm in arm with Evie. Her eyes met mine then fell to my arm in its cast, then shot back up to my eyes and I braced myself for her reaction.

"Do I even want to know?" she asked, her tone half concern, half exasperation.

"I was bitten by a shark," I said in a serious tone as I looked at her dead in the face.

She blinked, stared at my arm, stared right into my eyes and back at my arm again. "I knew it. I told you. I *told you!* How bad is it? Oh my god. You're lucky to be alive!"

I couldn't keep a straight face any longer. I burst into fits of laughter at her genuine concern.

"I'm joking, obviously. I broke my arm trying to hop over some rocks at the beach. No sharks involved. I wasn't even in the water. I'm okay. It's only a mild break. It's just a bit sore."

Her face collapsed for a moment and I could see genuine worry and upset shining from her gaze. "You never told me. Why didn't you tell me?"

"I didn't want you to worry while you were at the party. Besides, you promised me pictures of all your drinks in exchange for pictures of my injuries. I don't seem to remember getting any of those."

She looked down at her feet, her expression shuttering off her emotions to me. "Oh yeah, the party. I didn't really drink."

When she eventually looked back up, that sparkle in her eyes had darkened into nothingness.

"What? Why? Is Ollie okay?"

Her eyes rolled in a way that didn't look entirely indulgent. "He's loved up to the eyeballs."

"Oh. I guess that's good then." I tried reading her expression but it was impossible. She was a closed book that I desperately wanted to open. "So, no drinking at the party? What *did* you get up to?" I asked, trying to coach something other than a one word answer from her.

"Oh, you know… party stuff? How was your weekend apart from the sharks and rocks?"

"My weekend was good aside from spending some of it in A&E. Nice to be out on the waves but it's likely I won't be going back out there for a while." I couldn't comprehend how much I was going to miss surfing. I was going to need to get a new hobby and fast if I was going to survive. "Oh, speaking of parties… Alfie's having one in a couple of weeks and invited us. Only a select few people are going. Fancy it? You'll be able to have more fun doing *party stuff.*"

Her forehead creased at my mention of being out of the water for a little while but widened with what I thought was interest when I mentioned the party. Her head tilted when she asked, "Go… with you?"

I shuffled in one spot, fighting with my natural instinct to ask her along as a friend. "Well, yeah. I've been on a date with your dog so I thought the next logical step would be, I dunno…" I fought even more with my words and then blurted uncontrollably. "Me and you going to the party together? I could pick you up?"

She looked thoughtful for a moment and I was afraid she was going to say no. But then her shoulders firmed, her chin lifted and her jaw set as though she'd settled on a decision. "Yeah, okay," she said, her face splitting into a smile. "Sounds good."

"Great." I tried to play it casual when I felt anything but. "My arm should be a little better by then, too."

I could barely believe what I was hearing. I had a date with Lola Long. *A date*! My stomach did flips in celebration, and I barely kept my cool—if only I could keep it up for a couple of weeks until the party.

It was shameful to say that, for at least a week, I milked my broken arm in all aspects of my life. It came with rewards I couldn't stop reaping, like extra ice cream for dessert and all the fuss from friends and family, but more importantly, Lola, who couldn't do enough for me. We found more and more reasons to see each other, which included an evening at her house for films and a home cooked, nutritious meal.

As I walked into Lola's house, she straightened up my jacket and collar on my polo shirt. That was the trouble with having a broken arm. I could barely look after myself, so I was thankful for her. As she adjusted my collar, I felt her warm breath on my cheek, which made my skin flush, and as she pulled away, her fingers grazed my neck. Her touch was electrifying, sending shockwaves right through my body. All I wanted to do was wrap my arms around her and kiss her perfectly shaped lips. But I couldn't do that—under no circumstances was I going to scare her off.

"Thank you for having me over. Did you decide on a film?" I asked before following her into her lounge and being greeted by a very happy Dave.

"Oh my god, Dave, calm down," she said through a laugh, trying to drag the poor dog away to stop him from jumping up and licking my face. "I've got a couple of films queued up on the box that I thought you might like," she went on with a mischievous grin.

Then she grabbed the remote and flicked the telly on, beaming proudly at me as the two films sat there on the screen waiting. *The Meg* and *The Shallows*. Both shark movies.

"You're relentless. You know that, right? Why don't we watch something with fewer shark attacks? Why don't you put on your favourite film?"

She grinned, tapping the remote against her hand thoughtfully. "Just doing my duty as your... whatever. It's important that you know the dangers." I could tell she was goading me from the glint in her eyes as she spoke. "But if you wanna watch my favourite film, we can do that. It has fewer shark attacks... more dinosaurs."

Lola clicked the remote a couple of times to the recently watched section and hovered over Jurassic Park. I could have guessed. "You know I've never actually seen Jurassic Park?"

Her hand flew to her chest and she gasped and glared at me as though I'd just told her her dog was ugly. "You *what?*"

"I mean, it's my favourite film of all time, too," I said

sarcastically, hoping to avoid the remote control being launched at my bad arm.

"Sit your arse down," she ordered, leaning in to plump up the cushions for me, muttering something under her breath that sounded a lot like *uncultured swine*. "I'll get dinner on while you watch. I can quote the whole film from start to finish so I can drop in and out."

I blinked a couple of times and then replied with a salute and a smile. "As you command. What are we having for food?"

"Tonight, monsieur, we will be dining on succulent chicken breast, coated in free range eggs and the finest bread crumbs, deep fried in sunflower oil from the groves of Italy, served with earthy potatoes, sliced and lovingly home baked in the finest of ovens."

"Nice! I love how you've just managed to make chicken and chips sound fancy. You're so clever. Thanks Little-Legs."

She winked before shuffling off to the kitchen and proceeding to make shoving some chicken and chips onto baking trays sound like she was splitting the atom. Apparently, she'd been lying about being a domestic goddess.

Jurassic Park started and I concentrated, trying to take in every little detail in case there was a quiz at the end. Lola joined me on the sofa only a couple of loud crashes later.

My stomach growled in hunger, alerting both Dave and Lola, prompting her to shush me. I rubbed it with my good hand in an attempt to comfort it—it wouldn't be long until it was graced with the culinary masterpiece Lola was about to present it with.

An hour later, the dinosaurs were wreaking havoc on

Isla Nubla, and my stomach was still growling. It was hard to tell whether these were special breaded chicken pieces that took longer to cook, or Lola had just checked out of the cooking process altogether in favour of watching people get dismembered by prehistoric carnivores. Until the smoke alarm went off…

"Shit! Food!" Lola exclaimed, finally dragging her eyes away from the screen and legging it to the kitchen.

The incessant beeping of the smoke alarm she apparently used as an oven timer did eventually go quiet, and she shuffled into the room carrying a baking tray piled with what looked like charred remains. "Umm, so… what are your thoughts on takeaway pizza?" she asked sheepishly.

"I mean, they don't look too bad, do they?" I bravely took a piece of chicken off the baking tray and was about to place it in my mouth until Lola dropped the tray to the floor and knocked the burnt remains out of my hand. Dave ran over to the food that had fallen onto the floor, but even he turned his nose up at them. "Pizza it is then."

She stared at me for a long moment, a strange expression on her face before she eventually spoke. "You were gonna eat that? Just to be nice?"

"Well, yeah." I blushed as my left foot made invisible patterns on the floor.

"But… it was charcoal?"

"I'm sure it would have been tasty underneath the charcoal," I said and then winced a little as my shoulder ached. "You know the worst thing about having a cast? I can never get comfy and sleeping is proving difficult. It's so awkward to find a position where the rest of my body doesn't hate me. My back is absolutely killing."

"Oh…" Her eyes widened in alarm and she dropped down next to me, her fingers moving to my shoulder. "Is it bad? Can I… I don't know… do anything to help?"

"You can give me a massage. That would help."

"Right, umm…" She shifted in her seat, trying to manoeuvre herself to make herself taller than me, which was hilarious when knowing she was around five foot three in heels. "I can do that. I think? You might need to be less tall."

I must have gone bright red at the thought of her hands all over me, covered in lotion. I cleared my throat and then flustered, trying to find some words. "Umm. That would be good. I can. Umm. I'll sit."

I shifted onto the floor and Lola moved in behind me, her legs bracketing me in a way I tried not to think too hard about. Her fingers danced over my shoulders, hesitantly at first, as though she wasn't quite confident.

"So, what kind of pizza do you like?" she asked conversationally, reminding me of my growling stomach. "No pressure, but if you come down on the wrong side of the pineapple debate, it could be friendship ending."

"My favourite is pepperoni. Pineapple does not belong on pizza." I flinched and prepared for a blow to my shoulders just in case she was a lover of it.

She growled… *growled,* and jabbed a finger into my shoulder blade viciously. "Get out of my house." Despite her words, she carried on massaging, her fingers slowly gaining in confidence and working into some of the knots that sleeping awkwardly had tied in my muscles.

"Normally, I'd be worried I upset you, but those fingers of yours are making it very easy for me to not have a care in the world right now."

"Careful, Larson. You already have two strikes tonight. One more and no pizza for you."

"You've literally put the power in my hands by giving me your phone to order. I'd quit while you're ahead, Little-Legs."

She snorted, digging her thumb into a particularly tender spot. "If you order anything with sweetcorn or tuna on, I swear to god I will break your spine. Don't test me, buddy."

"Ouch!" I yelped out. "Have I ever told you how much I love this side of you?" I turned my neck to face her, our eyes meeting. She had that glisten back, and damn did they sparkle.

I felt something between us. A connection. Electricity. Pure lust. I would have wrapped my lips around hers right there and then. But I didn't.

I resisted temptation.

There was no way I was going to ruin this moment. I knew Lola wasn't like the other girls at school. She was gentle and kind.

Her kissing me wouldn't just be a kiss—it would be like her giving me a part of herself, and I was willing to wait. It didn't matter how long that took. I'd wait a whole lifetime as long as I had Lola in my life.

CHAPTER 15
LOLA

Everything was completely fine.

I had everything under control and there was absolutely nothing to get upset about.

Clearly.

All that talk with Hannah at the party has been a load of fuss over nothing. I'd got myself into a massive state, cried buckets of tears, made poor Dave listen to me ranting about trying to make it through life alone in this economy, slept for about twelve hours straight, then woken up and decided it was all rubbish and I was far too young to be putting labels on myself regardless.

Then I'd seen Noah's arm all screwed up from his surfing trip, and my heart had practically caved in when he'd joked about being attacked by a shark. It had become a standing joke between us now, my constant obsession with him being eaten by a shark. But behind the joke was a very real fear.

I didn't even like swimming in pools, where you could clearly see the bottom. And maybe I had seen too many disaster movies where people drowned, got devoured by sea monsters, or generally died in horrible ways at sea, but nothing could convince me that what he did most weekends was perfectly safe.

I already had half my brain power eaten up worrying about Ollie, who I hadn't spoken to since the party because I was far too ashamed about how I'd spoken to him. Now, I had the other half taken up with worrying about Noah being taken out by a kraken at the weekend, too.

These boys would be the death of me. Even though it felt like when Noah smiled at me or laughed at my terrible jokes, it gave me life. I'd even thought it might be okay when he'd looked at me as though he wanted to kiss me when I massaged his shoulders. I mean, sure, there was part of me that thought that all exchanges of bodily fluids were abhorrent, but maybe... with Noah, it might be okay.

Maybe it really was true what they said and you really did just have to wait to meet the right person.

I was busy overthinking everything while trying not to think by cleaning, an activity I usually avoided like the plague, rolling my eyes when I saw Mum's keys on the fireplace again. She was always forgetting them. Taylor Swift was blasting through the Bluetooth speaker in the corner and I was breaking out dance moves with my duster that would have made Mrs Doubtfire proud, when the doorbell ruined my perfect karaoke moment.

It would be Mum coming back for her keys, undoubtedly.

There was no need for her to press and hold the damn thing for so long, though. I yelled as much loudly at her as

I yanked the door open before recoiling at the sight of Ollie standing there where I'd expected my mum.

My forehead dipped instantly into a frown as I internally tried to work out how I felt seeing him there. Ashamed, embarrassed, and maybe a little hurt at how distant he'd become since he'd got together with Cade. It was hard not to feel a little bit abandoned when we'd always spent every spare moment together and now he'd moved on to something cuter. But this was Ollie, my best friend who I worried about every damn day. I wasn't going to let our friendship die over something that trivial. I just needed some time to work out what I wanted and where this thing with Noah was going to go before I spilled my guts to him.

It didn't come naturally to me, keeping things from him, but for now, it was how I needed it to be.

I felt kind of guilty when he apologised to me, knowing that I was the one who'd been rude and dismissive of him the night of the party. I wasn't proud of it and I let him know it.

By the time he left, an hour or so later, I felt like maybe I had my friend back.

In fact, considering my meltdown after the party, I had to admit that things were pretty good. For the next couple of weeks, I took care of Noah as much as I could, hanging out at my place most nights. We burned our way through all the Jurassic Park and Jurassic World films, along with a lot more supposedly fool-proof freezer foods that were sacrificed on the altar of my terrible cooking.

He and my mum mind-melded almost the moment they met. I'd hoped that her inner nurse would come out and that she'd give him grief about all the dangers of open water sports. In reality, they wound up ganging up on me about the fact that, allegedly, it was more dangerous to get in a car than it was to surf in British waters.

I really enjoyed being around him and was getting more and more comfortable in his company, but I swear my mum was obsessed with him. She'd ask constantly when he'd be over next and give me irritatingly knowing looks I didn't dignify with responses.

Things were good. Really good.

So, when Hannah texted me a few weeks after the party, asking how I was doing, I didn't have any difficulty replying that I was fine and yes, I'd love to meet up for a drink and a chat.

The bookshop in town was the obvious place. It was Ollie's favourite so I'd been there more times than I could count, and I knew they did the best coffee in town for Hannah and Pepsi Max for me.

It was a freezing cold day, one of those where the air hurts your face and makes your eyes sting. Hannah greeted me outside the bookshop wearing a thick woollen coat and a matching turquoise scarf and knitted hat with a big hug.

"How are you?" she asked with a warm smile in spite of the chill in the air.

"Good," I replied genuinely. "I'm really good. How about you?"

"Yeah, I'm okay. A little stressed out at the workload. A-levels are hard, right? Like, really hard?"

I thought guiltily of all the work I'd left undone that week in favour of hanging out with Noah and watching my favourite films again. "Uh, yeah, absolute nightmare. Never seems to end. What subjects are you taking?"

"Dance, drama, English and chemistry. My parents told me I couldn't do dance or drama unless I did academic subjects as well. I'm just lucky I get to perv on the chemistry teacher. She makes it a whole lot easier. What subjects do you do?"

"Wow, that sounds intense. I always called chemistry che-mystery for all the sense it made to me. I'm doing health and social care. It's full time so no A-levels. Thankfully. They sound vile."

"Chemistry is hard but Miss Locke somehow makes sense of it all for me. She speaks my language." Hannah's expression went vacant, like her spirit had run off with Miss Locke and left her body in the coffee shop.

I couldn't help wondering what it was like to get so dreamy over another person like that.

"I bet she does," I replied playfully, kicking her shin lightly under the table.

"She really does. God, my parents would kick off if they found out that was the only reason I chose chemistry. They're not going to be happy when I pick my university course and I leave chemistry and Miss Locke behind. That is unless I can convince her to run away with me before then."

I laughed, accepting my large Pepsi Max from the waitress and watching Hannah taking a sip from a giant cappuccino. "Surely they just want you to be happy, though, right? No point studying something you hate at uni."

"You've got to be kidding. They only want what looks good for them. My mum isn't so bad, but she just goes along with whatever my dad says because it's easier that way. I can't wait to move away if I'm honest. Maybe then

I'll catch my break." Hannah's usually infectious personality seemed to dim as she spoke about her parents.

"It kinda sounds like you want to be using some of that high level chemistry knowledge to poison your dad. I hear polonium is popular with the Russians. Something to think about." I grinned, hoping to bring the spark back into her expression, missing it already.

She snorted a laugh. "Find me a supplier and I'll make it happen."

"I'll see what I can do." I winked and took a sip of my drink. "So how are things apart from academic hell?"

"Alright, I guess. Nothing to report. What about you? The last time I saw you, things seemed to be a little rocky for you?"

My head ducks on my shoulders and I chew at my fingernail awkwardly, thinking of the party and how I left things. "Oh, yeah. All good. False alarm or whatever. I've got... I dunno feelings or something for this guy from college so I guess I can't be what you said. We have a date soon."

"Oh really? That's good, I guess. Although, did you even consider that you might be ace?"

Only incessantly for hours after we spoke.

"I mean sure, but Noah and I have been getting closer and I think I really like him so I'm obviously a boring old straight, aren't I?" I chuckled but the sound fell flat even to my ears.

"You clearly must be then. So, what base are you guys at? First? Second? Don't tell me you've already slept with him?" Hannah grinned, pressing on exactly the right nerve.

"Well, no, but I'm sure it's only a matter of time," I

replied in an attempt to brush off her question about bases. How was I meant to tell her that me and the guy I was basing my entire theory of straightness on hadn't done anything more than shameless flirting on my mum's couch while watching dinosaurs tear each other apart. I doubted she'd find it romantic.

I hated that feeling. The one of being somehow younger than people my own age just because I had less experience than them. I couldn't understand why somehow slotting genitals together was a symbol of being a 'proper grown up'.

"He's taking me to a party for our first date. Maybe it'll happen then. Who knows?" I tried to wiggle my eyebrows enticingly but all I could think was how unromantic it would be to lose my virginity to a quickie on a pile of coats in Alfie Wilson's spare room.

"Wow. Well, if it does happen, I want all the details. Minus details of his gross penis, of course. In the meantime, I dunno, maybe you should just give asexuality a Google?"

I shrugged, feigning nonchalance. "I guess I could. It's good to be informed, right?"

Secretly, I thought I probably agreed with her about penises being gross.

CHAPTER 16

NOAH

Those few weeks from bonfire night to December seemed to disappear quickly as I lived the run up to Alfie's party in a euphoric bubble. Nothing was going to pop it, not even my own self sabotaging ways. I had to pinch myself on my freshly plaster-free arm on multiple occasions just to make sure I wasn't living a dream.

In reality, Lola was coming with me to the party. Not as a friend, but as my date, and I couldn't wait to spend the night with her.

I pulled on a black shirt, open collar, and accompanied it with a pair of black jeans and black polished shoes I'd bought especially. A couple of sprays of my favourite aftershave later—the one that made Lola's nose twitch—and I was ready to leave the house to pick up my date. My Lola.

Mum was waiting at the bottom of the stairs, her eyes practically taking the shape of love hearts as she looked adoringly up at me.

"You look so handsome," she said through a smile it was rare to see her wearing.

It was enough to intensify the feeling of euphoria that rushed through my mind. I loved seeing her like this, and I tried not to let the worry that was pitted at the bottom of my stomach take over, because I knew that before long she'd be back to hiding from the world, unable to face day-to-day life.

"Thanks, Mum." I wrapped my arms tightly around her, giving her the warmest embrace I could. "Is Dad ready yet?"

"Not yet, he's just finishing up his tea. Are you sure you don't want something to line your stomach. I know how you kids get," she said out of concern, but I wasn't entirely sure I'd be able to keep any food down with my nerves pulsing so hard through my body. I might have spent time with Lola over the past week or so, but tonight was different. Tonight, she wasn't just my friend, and I hoped whole heartedly that tonight would be the start of the rest of our lives together.

"No, I'm fine. Alfie will have food at his house, and I'm not a kid anymore. I'm a man." I gave her a sarcastic smile and walked past her towards the dining room.

"You smell like a man, too. Bloody hell, Noah, how much of that aftershave have you sprayed?" She laughed and coughed simultaneously, choking on my scent.

"Not that much. Lola likes it."

"I'm sure she does, but you didn't need to bathe in it." She followed me through into the dining room and picked a banana from the fruit bowl. "Have this at least. You know how I worry."

Worry. She did worry. It was all she did. She didn't go a

single minute without battling her thoughts. I took the banana, hoping that she'd get in bed worrying a little less that evening.

"Ready, son?" Dad said in between mouthfuls.

"Yeah. You're not taking us like that, are you?" I said, judging the jogging bottoms splattered with paint, which he claimed were his comfy pants. "You're going to have to change. I'm not having Lola meet you looking like you've had a paint fight with a group of toddlers. Lola's dog will be better dressed than you at this rate."

Dad rolled his eyes, took another mouthful of lasagne, and got up from his chair. "Someone's feeling extra precious today," he said under his breath to Mum, her mouth turning upwards in an indulgent smile.

I didn't even try to muster a comeback. I just smiled at how happy they looked together. I wanted to love Lola as much as Mum and Dad loved each other. I wanted to be there for Lola on her worst days to try to make them brighter, and to be the reason for her favourite days—the ones where the sun is shining and the birds are singing and everything is good.

After I'd forced down the banana I didn't want, Dad came downstairs after changing, looking a little more presentable. "Does one approve?"

"Much better. Now, let's go before we're late." I wasn't going to give Lola any excuse to get out of this one. It was going to be perfect.

We pulled up outside Lola's house, and as Dad sat waiting in the car at the side of the road, I walked up to her front door. I must have stood in the cold for a minute or two before I heard the car window wind down and Dad shout, "Doors generally work better when you knock."

I glared at him before curling my hand into a fist, my fingers twitching with nerves.

But in reality, I didn't need to knock. Dave started barking and sniffing around, and before I knew it, the door was open and Lola stood dressed to impress. Her deep-purple sequin dress acted like a disco ball, reflecting light that danced right out into the street. Time slowed as I looked at her, seeing stars and nothing else, other than Dave running around my ankles, jumping excitedly up to the carrier bag that did not compliment my outfit one bit.

I knelt down to Dave, mussing up the fur on the top of his head, and then presented him with a peace offering. A salmon fillet, cut and prepared by the fishmonger himself. Only the best for Dave, as Lola would have said.

"Here you go. I couldn't come empty handed when I'm stealing away your favourite human now, could I?" I continued stroking Dave and looked up to Lola and her smiling face.

"I'm glad to see that you're on board with the whole spoiling Dave rotten plan," she said with a grin. "Consider the 'stealing his human' tax paid in full."

"I'm very glad. You look... Wow." I could feel my face blushing and hoped the cold wind would at least take some of the blame.

Her own cheeks coloured slightly and she looked down at her dress, looking a combination of pleased and embarrassed. "Thank you. I brushed my hair and everything. Special occasion and all." She winked and attempted to drag Dave back inside, apparently against his will from the protest he put up. "Shall we?"

"Absolutely. By the way, I apologise in advance for anything my dad says."

"I heard that. That's the magic of an open window. Lola, nice to meet you. I'm Mr Larson, but you can call me Jeff." His face was a shade of serious.

I opened the passenger seat door for Lola, and minding her dress, she stepped in. "Nice to meet you, Jeff."

Dad burst into a fit of laughter and I rolled my eyes. "His name is Ian, and Ian clearly thinks he's hilarious when really his is the worst excuse for comedy, ever."

Chuckling, she shifted around in the seat, tucking her short, flirty dress under her legs. "Come on. That was quality comedy content," she argued in my dad's favour.

"You don't have to be nice to him just because he's my dad, you know?" I said to Lola and then scowled at my dad in the rear view mirror where he was looking pretty pleased with himself.

"I have feelings, too, you know?" he said, trying to make another funny. According to Lola, apparently he was a hit.

"What are we still doing at Lola's? Drive. Get us to the party already."

And so he did, telling dad jokes the whole way to Alfie's house. He even asked questions, trying to get to know Lola, and although I wouldn't tell him, he was surprisingly well behaved—even asking things he already knew to cover up how much I'd chewed my parents' ears off about her.

A short car journey later and our legs saved from a long walk in the cold, I hopped out of the car first, running to the other side to open the door for Lola.

"Have fun you two. No funny business. This is your first date, remember?" Dad laughed and my face screwed up at the sight of Lola's cheeks turning the brightest shade of red.

Correction. My dad *had been* on his best behaviour.

"Leave. Now." I gave him daggers, and then my expression softened slightly. "And, thank you for the lift. I appreciate it. Now, leave."

Lola linked arms with me, leaning into me ever so slightly as we walked up Alfie's driveway towards his house. "Again, I'm so sorry about my dad. He clearly thinks he's extra funny today." Lola laughed and shook her head, seeming unfazed by his humour. "Thank you for being my date for the party. I'm over the moon I get to have a girl like you on my arm."

She glanced over at me, and for a moment it looked like there was a joke on the tip of her tongue, but when she saw my earnest expression, her eyes softened and instead she simply said, "Thank *you* for inviting me."

We stepped into Alfie's house, but it seemed different to normal. There were half as many people as there usually were, the lounge furniture wasn't pushed to the edge of the room and instead, sat proudly in the centre, with festive cushions placed on them. The house was Santa's Grotto on acid, but it somehow worked with the high ceilings and clean white decor of the house.

"Yo, Noah's here. And Lola, too." Alfie's hand reached out to high five me, which turned into the typical awkward bro handshake he did with everyone he considered a friend. A few of the others waved to Lola and I, and we were quickly met with drinks. They were called Alfie's Festive Cocktail—apparently, a concoction of any and every spirit that looked or sounded christmassy.

After we'd all necked a few of the cocktails laced with an aniseed flavour, it was that time again.

"Let's play drinking games," Alfie yelled, and agreement echoed off the walls. It wasn't like we needed any more alcohol. I was already seeing Lola in slow motion after drinking cocktails far too quickly purely out of nerves. But, we were going to play games; there was no choice in the matter. That being said, I couldn't deny my excitement especially as Lola was here. It was a bit of harmless fun. All we needed was a single card and our mouths.

CHAPTER 17
LOLA

It was the weirdest night. I felt like I was somehow outside of myself, looking down and watching the evening unfolding. With the strongest punch I'd ever tasted buzzing through my veins and Noah sat beside me looking as giddy as though he'd won the lottery, when in reality, all that had happened was that I'd gone on a date with him. I had to admit that having somebody so excited to spend time with you did not suck. At all. Especially when that someone was Noah Larson, with his blond curls and sparkling eyes as blue as the ocean on a summer's day.

Eventually, I found myself sitting cross-legged on the carpet between Evie and Noah like I was back at primary school and ready for show and tell. Except this was sixth form show and tell and it involved alcohol, a playing card and a lot more kissing than I was generally comfortable with.

The purpose of the game appeared to be to pass the card from person to person around the circle using only your lips. Without the alcohol zinging around my system, it was the sort of game I'd definitely have rejected, but there I was, part of the circle and ready to play.

I watched curiously as the card started its rounds, half dreading the moment it would get to me. Unsurprisingly, when it got to Alfie, he 'accidentally' dropped it, which apparently meant he then had to kiss the person he'd been about to pass it on to. Anita Rayworth: apparently his new conquest. The entire process appeared kind of awkward and highly unsanitary to me, but I observed with interest and no small amount of panic anyway.

Would Noah want to kiss me? I'd never kissed anybody before. Would he be able to tell how inexperienced I was? Should I have told him before I got myself into this situation in the first place?

Anxious thoughts and questions battered around my brain, fighting for dominance and keeping me from learning anything about good kissing technique from Alfie and Anita. Besides, their kiss seemed to be over before it had begun, and judging by the unamused expression on Anita's face, maybe they weren't the couple to watch for tips.

When the card finally made its way around to me, I held onto that thing like my life depended on it. I probably burst a few blood vessels in the attempt, but I really wasn't sure I wanted my first kiss to be part of a game in the middle of a room full of people.

It seemed that Noah had other ideas, though. He didn't look remotely sorry when the card fluttered to the ground from his lips, the ace of hearts staring up at me in challenge.

"Come on then, Little-Legs," Noah said coaxingly, as

he tugged me gently closer to him until his breath fanned over my face.

His lips were surprisingly soft when they collided with mine. A cacophony of emotions roared through me, and warm shivers danced down my skin when his fingers softly caressed my jaw before tangling with my hair.

I had no thoughts for technique or experience in that moment. All there was in the world was Noah—this boy who seemed, unaccountably, to *like*-like me. He was everywhere and everything all at once, and I was lost to the sensation of him. My heart swelled and left me breathless when he finally pulled away, his fingers dancing lightly, thoughtfully, over his lips while I could do nothing but stare at him.

"Damn, Larson!" Alfie's voice reached me through the haze my brain had turned into, and the assembled group began to chatter loudly amongst themselves while Noah and I remained locked in our own bubble, our eyes zoomed in only on each other. He was all I could see in the world, and based on his expression, it was the same for him with me.

Several more glasses of toxic punch later and I was beyond buzzed and well into drunk territory. Noah hadn't left my side all evening, and the more time I spent with him, the more I wanted to spend to spend all my future minutes and hours with him. He was funny, clever and charming, and when we danced together, his hands skimmed my waist and his lips danced over my forehead in a way that had goosebumps erupting all over my skin.

Even attempting to navigate the stairs following a bathroom visit was twice the usual fun, since the stairs seemed to have multiplied, and where sober me would have seen one, party me saw three. Picking the right one each time became a game, and I allowed myself a little mini wave and whoop of celebration for each step I managed without breaking my neck.

"Somebody looks pleased with themselves," a familiar voice said playfully when I finally reached the bottom.

At least, I thought it was the bottom. The wooden hallway floor looked decidedly wobbly to me so there was no guarantee I'd actually found flat land.

"Did the stairs; didn't die," I announced proudly to Evie, who was standing watching with a wide, amused smile.

"Congratulations," she played along, laughing slightly. "Though I'd have thought you were congratulating yourself on other successful conquests tonight."

I blinked at her, both in confusion and trying to work out which version of her was the real one. There were at least three that I could see.

"You... huh? Oops!" Reaching for the wrong Evie to throw my arm over the shoulder of, resulted in me accidentally hitting her in the boob and then somehow falling right to the floor, creased up with giggles.

"You okay down there?" Evie asked, full on laughing now. "How much punch have you had?"

I grabbed onto the closest version of her hand as it waved helpfully in front of me, and instead of allowing her to help me up, I tugged on it instead, pulling her closer to me and whispering conspiratorially, "More than a little but not as much as a lottle. Punch gives me courage."

"I'll say," she said through a chuckle. "You want some help up?"

I patted the ground I was sitting on quite contentedly

and said, "Nope," popping the P petulantly. "Can you tell Noah I live here now? It's nice here. It has this little pillow for my head, see?"

"That's the stairs, hun," she deadpanned. "But I'll tell Larson where you… Never mind. Here he is now."

I looked up eagerly and Noah's beautiful face swam into view, in radiant four-way technicolour. I didn't even try to work out which version was the real one. I just basked in the image of four of him at once and whispered loudly to Evie, "He's nice, you know? And he kissed me earlier."

Looking perplexed by my inability to realise that he could hear every word I was saying, she stage whispered back, "I know. I saw. We all saw. And I hate to say I told you so but…"

"That's right. You did." I grinned when Noah sat down beside me and instinctively reached for my hand. "Noah, this is Evie. She's a time travelling fortune teller."

"Is she now?" His eyebrow quirked and his voice cracked in amusement.

"No, honey," she said, patting my other hand patronisingly. "I just have eyes." She glanced between the two of us with a satisfied smile before standing up and pointing over her shoulder, back towards the party. "I'll leave you two to it."

Then she was gone and I was alone with the boy whose kisses made my stomach do flip flops. His thumb was brushing lightly over the back of my hand as we both stared at the point of contact.

"Hi," I said dopily, looking up and staring into what I hoped was the right set of bright blue eyes.

"Hey, you. Want some company?" he said, nudging me playfully and wearing the biggest smile.

"Depends," I replied. "Is it yours?"

"I thought that went without saying." He gave a little chuckle and then wrapped his fingers around mine, making me feel somehow warm and protected all at once. "It's a great party, isn't it?"

"Mmm," I hummed, patting the step behind me. "This is where I live now. Do you like it? It has a pillow built in. We could lie here and watch the stars."

Noah's smile was still beaming even through a look of bemusement as I slurred my words. "It's lovely. Really... white. I would have thought you'd have decorated a little differently. But, I guess being even drunker than I am, you haven't had time."

"Ssssshhhhh," I said loudly, covering my mouth with my finger. "Don't tell anybody I'm drunk. S'a secret."

"I think you being drunk is about as obvious and as talked about as our kiss before."

I giggled like a little kid, or one of those girls I hated for being stupid over guys. "I never played that game before." I attempted to reach for his face but missed and my hand landed on his chest instead where I could feel his heart beating steady and strong. "Have you?"

"Nope," he said, before looking down at his shiny pair of shoes. "But, now that I have, I think it's my favourite."

"I didn't think I'd like kissing." The drunken words slurred out of me regardless of what sober me would have liked to keep secret. "But with you, it was... mmmm." I grinned and touched my lips with my free hand.

"The kiss was something." Noah paused for a minute, deep in thought. I wondered if he was picturing kissing me again. "Anyway. How's about we go dance before our night is over and your mum comes to pick us up?"

"Oooh yes, dancing. Need to text Mum a time first. Forgot about that. Where's my phone?" I patted down my dress, locating my phone in my pocket and attempting three times to unlock it before I was successful. Opening the message stream with my mum, I cringed when I saw that there was already an unopened message there from her. "Uh oh!"

"What's up? Realised you'll have to leave your newly found, undecorated home on these steps and go to your actual home?" Noah laughed through a smirk. He seemed funnier through my intoxicated eyes.

"Actually, we might have to stay. Mum got called into work. We really do live here now." I cringed apologetically, some of the drunken buzz lifting from my mind at my mum's message.

"Oh no. I can get us a taxi if you want? It's probably a bit late to call Dad, and Mum will just worry."

I stared at him, enjoying the way I seemed to fall right into those eyes of his, and realised that no matter how long this night went on, it would never be long enough for me. "We could walk?" I suggested hopefully. "Like last time."

"Yeah, that'd be nice. Like our own little tradition. Won't you be cold, though? It's freezing out."

"Nah," I assured him, grinning and lifting my arm, flexing my muscle as though it was something special. "I'm well hard, innit?"

"Okay, now I know you're definitely more drunk than me. Come on, Little-Legs. Let's have a dance before we have to go." Noah hopped up from the step and held out his hand ready to pull me up.

"Oh, kind sir, I do declare you're such a gentleman," I slurred in my best, yet still somehow terrible, impression of a Deep South American accent. Then I took his hand and allowed him to pull me up to standing, throwing my arms around his neck, partly to be close to him and partly to steady myself before I tumbled over again.

Our breaths intertwined as our eyes locked just inches from each other. "I don't know whether that's your aniseed breath or mine, but I like it."

Beaming, I brushed a kiss against his cheek before whispering in his ear, "I like *you*. Let's dance, shark boy."

And I dragged him back into the party where the two of us attracted some interested looks and several wolf whistles. I stiffened a little when I realised what people thought we'd been doing while we were gone, but I stored my reaction to that away in that box of things I chose not to think about and slammed the lid down hard.

For now, I was a normal teenage girl at a party, dancing with the boy she liked who seemed to like her back, and who she enjoyed kissing. Nothing else mattered.

About an hour later, out in the cold on the road home, I enjoyed the feel of our hands entwined swinging between us as we talked.

"I don't care if it's for kids or not. I want to go on the Polar Express," I insisted loudly, stumbling over a rock on the pavement and enjoying the feel of his body next to mine when he saved me from falling.

"The Polar Express is not for kids, and if you end up getting your hand on tickets, you better take me with you." Noah's expression was dead serious until his mouth turned upwards and he started laughing. "Speaking of

Christmas, I can't believe how quickly it's come round. What are your plans?"

I shrugged. Christmas in the Long household tended to be something of a haphazard affair. It really all depended on my mum's working pattern, and with things as they were in the NHS, her working pattern those days seemed to be almost all the time. "Not much probably. If Mum's working, it'll probably consist of me and Dad sitting on the couch eating pigs in blankets from the packet in front of the Call the Midwife Christmas special and then cracking open the selection boxes. If she's not working, you can probably throw in a turkey, too. Dad's cooking skills are about as good as mine. How about you? Big family affair?"

"Well, I'd take your Christmas Day over mine. We always plan a big do. My brother comes over and we always plan to have the picture perfect Christmas: presents, enough food to feed an entire village and then board games with the family. In reality, it never works out. It's a really tough time of year for Mum and honestly, I'd go without all the Christmas shenanigans if it meant she could have another good day. Mum never compromises. Christmas is a day she's never willing for us to give up on when, in her words, we've had to sacrifice so much for her OCD. Honestly, it's a price we're all willing to pay." Noah's eyes weren't sparkling anymore. Instead, they were filled with sadness. His hand moved swiftly to wipe a lone tear from his eye before he tried his best to change the subject. "Call The Midwife? I'd always pegged you as a Doctor Who kind of gal."

I squeezed his hand and smiled sadly. I had to admit that I'd never really understood the impact OCD could have on so many parts of people's lives. Yet nobody really talked about it. Other conditions, people ran races for, or climbed mountains. Held coffee mornings or non-uniform days in schools. But it seemed like people with OCD were just kind of expected to get on with it. Them and their families.

"I'm sorry, Noah. That's so unfair. For you guys and your mum. For what it's worth, any of you would be welcome to couch surf with my dad and me. We can even watch Doctor Who if you like, though I kind of lost my way once David Tennant left."

"Didn't we all? No one can compare, although I did start watching it again when Jodie Whittaker became The Doctor. She's so..." His words trailed off as if he'd forgotten he wasn't talking to one of his guy mates.

"She's so...?" I prompted, grinning and nudging his shoulder with mine. "Don't hold back on my account."

"Hot. But you're *smoking* hot. Like at least four levels above her," he said smoothly, trying to dig himself out of a hole he'd dug all by himself.

I laughed so hard I had to bend double to contain it. "Relax. You're allowed celeb crushes. You're so adorable, though. It's a shame our first kiss was part of a game, don't you think?"

Noah coughed a little. "First kiss... You mean there's gonna be a second?"

My feet shuffled awkwardly as I glanced down at them. "I mean, only if you want there to be."

"Definitely. Very much so," he said without hesitation. His arm pulled me into him and both of them wrapped around me, shielding me from the cold wind.

There, in the circle of his arms, I felt invincible, like

nothing and nobody could ever hurt either of us. Popping up onto my tiptoes, I nudged his nose with mine and whispered, "What about a second-first kiss? Not because of a game, just because we want to?"

"I think that's a very good idea." Noah's fingers ran through my hair a couple of times before his hand caressed the back of my head and waited there until our lips trembled against each other's.

I must have watched a thousand romantic films over the years. The ones where the girl's foot pops when she's kissed by the Right Guy. Scenes with soaring music on cliff tops at sunset when the couple finally get that kiss you've waited the whole film for. But for me, that gentle kiss in the street, while he did his best to shield me from the cold, was worth a million of those fake movie scenes. His hands, his lips, and the warmth of his body next to mine were everything, and I knew that *this* was the first kiss that mattered. And that I would happily have a thousand more first kisses with him. We both shivered as the sky broke open and snowflakes began to fall, and without hesitation, I leaned in for first kiss number three.

CHAPTER 18
NOAH

"Merry Christmas, Mum." I wrapped my arms around her and immediately felt her tense up. "Do you need a hand with anything?"

She was already in the kitchen, mithering over a turkey before I'd even had a chance to grab my morning coffee.

"No, sweetie. That's okay. Go and keep your dad company. He's in the living room," she said without breaking eye contact with the turkey, clearly already worked up.

She'd been in surprisingly good spirits the day before, right up until the moment Nate messaged the family chat to say he'd be bringing his new girlfriend for Christmas. They'd practically only just started dating and, of all days, he thought he'd introduce her to the whole family on Christmas Day.

Absolutely ideal.

It wasn't all bad. I was eager to meet the woman who had enough patience to put up with Nate. She had to be virtually a saint.

But because Nate lacked any basic consideration for anyone but himself, we were left with a Mum who was determined to go to the ends of the Earth and back for us to have the perfect Christmas, when in fact, all we ever wanted was for her to be okay.

She didn't need to put so much pressure on herself; the change in routine always hit her harder than at any other time of the year.

Why *couldn't* Christmas be a mess? Why was it normal for everyone to speak about their expensive gifts and moist turkeys rather than the family fights over a flipped Monopoly board or the drunken uncle who used Christmas as an excuse for his excessive drinking?

I knew why.

I just hated it.

I'd spent most of my childhood pretending I'd had the best Christmases out of embarrassment, and just avoiding the subject matter at all costs the rest of the time.

Christmas in the Larson household was different, and that was okay.

"Happy Christmas, son," Dad said, sitting in his usual armchair wearing a white shirt and a tinsel tie.

"Merry Christmas. You know Mum's already looking mighty stressed in there?"

"I know." Dad's voice softened, sadness sweeping across his face. "You know we've got to leave her to it. She won't take no for an answer." I could tell Dad felt as helpless as I did, but he was right. If there was one thing having OCD didn't take away from her, it was her determination. She was strong enough and powerful enough to beat it, until she wasn't. She'd never quit, until she really had to. That was our mum, and boy did I love her for it.

I wondered if Mum would ever be powerful enough to admit that she was struggling, or manage another trip to the doctors. If she ever did, that would be the day when she was at her toughest, because her strength would be in admitting that she needed help. It would also be the day when I couldn't physically love her any more.

I heard Nate come barreling through the front door, half expecting to see his shoes fly past the living room doorway as he'd normally slam dunk them on the shoe rack. Instead, he walked past, sensibly placing two pairs of shoes neatly upon the rack.

I looked at Dad and he looked back at me, both of us sharing the same expression of bewilderment.

"Father. Noah. This is Emma." Nate introduced his new girlfriend, who walked into the living room with a sincere smile.

Who the hell was he? What had she done to my incessantly annoying brother?

"Emma, lovely to meet you." I shook her hand and then swiftly moved on to my brother. "Nathaniel, it's very good to meet you, too. Father, shall we prepare the many drinks? I can assure you, there will be a deluge of Prosecco in just one moment," I said, trying not to laugh and disguising my normal voice with my best Downton Abbey impression, but was met with a slap to the back of my head.

Knew he wouldn't be able to resist.

"It's wonderful to meet you both. Ian, I've heard you've got a cracking sense of humour. And well, Noey?" She looked at Nate, who gave Emma a reassuring nod. "I have a good feeling about you. I can't wait to hear all the stories about your brother. I've met many people in my life and read many books, but your brother's story is one I can't particularly understand. Maybe you'll be able to help me piece it together?"

I grinned and winked.

My brother glanced at her in horror. "You were supposed to be on my side."

"Oh, honey. I never take sides." She pressed a kiss on his cheek, making him blush brighter than I did around Lola. I thought I was bad but watching him take a few seconds to fully shake off the pure lust made me realise everything I felt for Lola was normal. Oh god, they were going to name us the love sick Larson brothers.

"Let me introduce you to Mum." Nate led Emma into the kitchen and I followed behind.

I watched her flustered appearance change in an instant as she hugged Emma. To an unknowing person, Mum was just like anyone else, but to the trained eye, you could see her hands and fingers shaking as she hugged her son's girlfriend. I could see the worry on her face and the redness of her eyes, knowing that she'd have spent the past few minutes completely breaking down while her family tried to carry on as normal around her, for her.

I looked to the floor, struggling to hide the sorrow that had become apparent on my face—not even the awkward, socially incoherent Nate could cheer me up.

So I texted the one girl I'd once tried to escape by visiting the seaside and surfing—the one person I never wanted to escape from again.

> Merry Christmas, Little-Legs. How's your festive day started? x

I didn't bother waiting for a reply. I knew that Lola would be spending time with her mum before her shift at the hospital. I had bought her the greatest gift for Christmas. I'd spent ages finding her the right present, because it had to be right. It was our first Christmas together as boyfriend and girlfriend. We'd not labelled it as such, but I guessed the kissing decided that for us.

"Connect Four?" My brother nodded my way, pulling the game from a carrier bag.

Every year he'd pull out a different game we could all play. Last year, it had been Battleships, and I'd failed miserably. The year before it had been Guess Who, and Dad had taken the win. This year was my year; it had to be.

Mum never played. She was always too caught up in the kitchen.

"Mrs Larson, are you coming to play?" Emma yelled through to the kitchen. Mum walked into the dining room, glanced at the game and then to Emma's pleading face.

Out of the corner of my eye, I saw Nate making failed attempts at signalling to Emma that she wouldn't play—that it was probably better this way.

"I guess I've got a few minutes," Mum said. I had to scrape my jaw off the ground in shock.

So, we played.

We took it in turns, the winner of each game moving onto the next round and the loser eliminated. I even caught Mum smiling indulgently at the competitiveness between Nate and Emma.

We must have talked and laughed through the games for around forty minutes, with the smoke alarm interrupting the final. Mine and Nate's competitive stares turned to looks of worry as we watched the fun drain right out of Mum, her expression turning to panic.

She jumped up in a fluster and ran into the kitchen. Dad followed, but not before holding up his index finger, signalling for us to stay exactly where we were.

"Should we go and help?" Emma asked over the muffled cries from the kitchen.

"No, we're best waiting here," Nate said, nodding in my direction, his expression checking if I was okay.

I nodded back, even though I wasn't okay. I was torn in half. Part of me despised Nate for bringing Emma, knowing the added pressure it would bring. But if Emma hadn't come, she wouldn't have played the game with us and it had been years since we'd seen a smile from Mum on Christmas Day.

Dad appeared around the corner, shaking his head. "Frozen lasagne, anyone?"

"What?" Nate and I both replied in unison.

"Best not to ask questions."

I didn't need to ask questions. I knew exactly what had happened because it happened almost every year.

"Lasagne sounds great." Emma smiled. "Are the semi-finalists having a rematch?"

> Merry Christmas, Shark Boy! One selection box down, and I'm starting on the next. Santa Claus the Movie on telly and Dad's already snoring on the couch. How's your day? x

The text from Lola came through shortly after I claimed the title of champion of Connect Four. And, to my surprise, Nate didn't sulk once. Boy, Emma really did have him in a love chokehold.

I smiled at Lola's message and sent her a picture of the burnt turkey, covered with all the trimmings, sitting proudly in the kitchen bin.

> Does this answer your question? x

Since the Christmas feast had ended up going to waste, Mum had taken herself upstairs to sit in her bedroom and Dad had taken over heating up the frozen lasagnes out of the freezer that had been placed there not too long ago for a rainy day—and well, it couldn't get rainier.

> Ooooh that does not look good. You okay? x

> Yeah. To be fair, it's not been the worst Christmas we've ever had. Finally met Nate's girlfriend, too. He's totally punching. I can't lie, though, I'm totally just wishing away the day. It's not worth all the stress x

> So that's two Larson lads who are punching, huh? ;) Plenty of space on our couch if you need sanctuary. The pigs in blankets are in the oven as I type and we're moving on to The Muppet's Christmas Carol in a minute. You're very welcome! x

I contemplated Lola's message for a second before replying. I *was* punching with Lola—in my eyes, she was the whole package. And because of that, I knew her offer of escape was sincere and not an empty gesture. She was the kind of person who would go to the ends of the Earth for anyone, not just for me—kindness was buried deep in her bones.

The thought of leaving my family and retreating to the comforting surroundings of Lola's place left me battling with an overwhelming feeling of guilt.

I couldn't leave, could I?

I walked into the living room to see Emma and Nate snuggled in front of the television, and Dad was upstairs with Mum.

I had no one.

Nate was all grown up and all loved up, and I'd have done anything to be in his shoes.

So I did.

I slipped on my shoes, looked in the mirror to make sure I looked reasonably well presented before yelling, "I'm going to Lola's house. Merry Christmas!" and then stepped out of the house.

Bracing against the cold, I shut the front door and began the walk to Lola's. I still felt the guilt rattling around in my stomach like a criminal trying to escape from prison, but I knew it was temporary.

It was temporary because the minute Lola opened her front door to me, everything bad I felt faded. Suddenly, nothing mattered but her.

"Hey, you," she crooned, leaping forward and yanking me into a tighter hug than she should have been capable of at her size. "You okay?"

"All the better for seeing you," I said, almost cringing at my own cheesiness, but it was true. "Thank you for rescuing me."

She grinned as she pulled back, grabbing my hand and

dragging me inside. "Well, me and Dad couldn't eat all these pigs in blankets alone anyway. We also have an abundance of cheese and a massive trifle Mum made before she got called into work at the last minute." She led me through to the living room where a man who looked like an older, male version of Lola was sitting with his feet propped up on the coffee table, a bowl of pigs in blankets resting on his chest. "Dad, this is Noah. Noah, this is my dad."

"Well damn," her dad said, grabbing the bowl and setting it on the table as he stood up to shake my hand. "Noah, is it? Never thought I'd see the day our Lollipop would bring home a fella who wasn't Ollie. It's nice to meet you, young man."

"Nice to meet you, too, sir." I fought my nerves and shook his hand as firmly as I could.

"Please, call me Rob. Make yourself at home, lad. We're not exactly having the most glamorous Christmas ever, but we've got the king of Christmas foods and the king of Christmas films so I reckon we're doing okay, right, Lolly?"

"Too right. Now, Noah, not to pile pressure on you or anything, and I'm not saying that the future of our entire relationship rests on your response to this question or anything, but... which is the greatest Christmas film of all time?"

I debated her question for a few seconds before announcing the Christmas film I'd grown up with. "It has to be *Home Alone 2: Lost In New York*." I'd always pictured going to New York and visiting all the places featured in the film. It looked so magical at Christmas.

Lola's dad sucked in air through his teeth as though

somebody had sustained a serious injury, shaking his head and slapping me lightly on the shoulder. "Tumbled at the first hurdle. Pity. I thought I was going to like you as well, Noah. Shame."

Lola laughed and knocked his hand away from me, tugging me down to sit on the couch between the two of them. "Not a bad effort, but we're about to rock your world with the true Greatest of all Time. Help yourself to snacks." She grabbed the remote to start the film queued up on the screen: *The Muppet's Christmas Carol.*

The film started and I sat with my stomach in knots as I waited for something to go wrong, the tension of which had me on the edge of my seat.

But nothing did. The pigs in blankets were cooked to perfection, the film was endurable and I didn't want to believe it but the weight from my shoulders seemed to melt away as I relaxed. For the first time on Christmas Day, I felt something other than anxiety.

It was paradise.

The mothership of all Christmasses.

I didn't get the present I'd wished for ever since I was young—something Santa couldn't ever bring or get his elves to make. All I'd ever wanted was for Mum to have a good day at Christmas.

This Christmas, I got a present I'd only ever dreamed of. I looked down at Lola smiling contentedly, her head resting in my lap as I played with her straight black hair, and I counted my lucky stars that I had her for Christmas.

CHAPTER 19
LOLA

Sandy Crew Group WhatsApp chat:

ALFIE:

Guys, disaster has struck! My parents have decreed that this is, in fact, their house and that if they want to have a New Year's Eve party here for their boring old friends who will all be in bed by midnight then they will! Can you believe the actual audacity? :(

Naturally, once Alfie's message came through, the chat immediately blew up with messages of disappointment and complaint. Predictably, nobody seemed to be willing to offer anything that so much as resembled a solution. Mind you, I thought, as I looked around my tiny terraced house, I wasn't exactly in a position to be of much help either. Unless…

I ignored the incessant pinging from the group chat

and opened up my messages with Ollie, smiling again at the string of hilarious memes he'd sent me just the previous day before trying to figure out how to word my message.

> Sooooooo, you know you love me and how even though you've defected to the dark side, your heart still lies at Sandford? Xx

> What you after, Long? lol

> Who says I have to be after anything?

> Long experience? You forget that I know you!

> Okay, fine, you got me. I'm begging favours. But actually it's Cade I need a favour from. What do you reckon are the chances of him hosting a party at his place on New Year's Eve?

He didn't reply instantly and I sighed, assuming the worst. But then my screen flashed with the words:

Ollie has added Cade to the chat.

The little box at the top of the chat told me Cade was typing and I held my breath, waiting and hoping. I wasn't sure why the New Year's Eve party was suddenly so important to me. Maybe it was because this year I finally had a boyfriend and I wanted to see the new year in with him. Either way, Cade's message seemed massively important as I waited for it to ping up on the screen.

CADE:

Did somebody mention a New Years Eve party? I mean, I'm already having a *whisper it* small gathering. Do you wanna come?

Cade! Love of my life, sweet, sweet bloke who makes my bestie soooooo very happy! How would you feel about turning your *whisper it* small gathering into a *shout it from the rooftops* party? Alfie's parents have reclaimed their house for an adult affair with quiet lift music, canapés and pearls, which has left the Sandy Crew in a bit of a pickle. And now you're madly in love with Ollie, that makes you at least 30% Sandy. So whadya think? Obvs we'll do all the work. We just need a venue!

I mentally repeated the word please over and over in my head as I watched the screen, waiting for him to type and desperately hoping.

CADE:

Hmmm. I do love a *shout it from the rooftops* party. What do you think about this Ollie? Is Lola at the point of desperation or do we make her beg some more?

OLLIE:

I mean, as fun as it is to watch Lolz grovelling and begging, I honestly don't care whether it's whispered or shouted as long as I get to kiss you at midnight!

Dude, gross!

> Or, you know, completely lovely and just what a best friend wants to hear. Obviously.

OLLIE:

> Nice attempt at saving yourself there, Lolz. For the first message, we will make sure we're right in your eye line every time we make out. All evening. Start the new year the way we intend to go on, I reckon. What do you think, Cade?

CADE:

> Sounds pretty damn good to me. Okay, I'm in. Rally the Sandy Crew!

> Oh my god I could kiss you! Don't worry, I won't. I'll get him to do it instead. I doubt I'll hear much complaining! lol. Thank you so much! You won't regret it. It'll be the greatest *shout it from the rooftops* party ever!

CADE:

> There will be no complaining from me either. I'll have all the Ollie kisses. The party will be great. Of course it will. It's one of mine ;)

Excited to be the bearer of good news, I hopped back over to the Sandy Crew group chat and typed so fast I had to keep deleting and retyping in my haste.

> Guys, I have a solution! Cade Wingate, Ollie's boyfriend, has agreed to host the party at his place. And, no offence, Alfie, but his house is RIDICULOUS! It'll be perfect! :D

Of course, the chat exploded with messages again, but there was only one name I was really interested in seeing on my screen.

Noah didn't reply straight away, and I found myself impatient to talk to him. I knew he wasn't practising his role as shark bait that weekend so hopefully he'd be near his phone when I messaged him privately.

> Sooooooo, it looks like I'm in need of a date for New Year's Eve. Know anybody who might fancy the job? xx

PICK ME! Just seen the messages in the group chat. Look at you being a regular hero xx

> Consider yourself picked! I mean, technically Cade is the hero. But if it wins me hero points anyway, who am I to argue? Can't wait for midnight. Next year is shaping up to be pretty awesome! xxx

You're telling me. Feel so lucky that I get to see the New Year in with you and escape the lack of celebrations in my own home. Bonus that I get to see Cade's house too. As much as I think Alfie will be happy to still be partying, I reckon he's going to hate not being host. He loves the limelight. Oh actually, you didn't really tell me much about the last party you went to at Cades. It was Bonfire Night, wasn't it? xxx

I stiffened at his question, my mind casting back to that party that seemed so long ago, but in reality had only been about two months ago. I thought back over the conversation I'd had with Hannah. That word: Asexual. But here I was, in a relationship with a gorgeous boy who unaccountably seemed to like me as much as I liked him. True, the thought of physical intimacy still sent anxiety cutting through me like a knife, but I imagined it was like that for everyone. I mean, it was a big step, wasn't it? Going all the way. I was certain that when the time was right, the anxiety would go away and I'd be over the moon to be with Noah in every single way.

> Oh, yeah, it was the night Ollie and Cade got together. Cade throws one hell of a party! Great snacks. xx

> We do love snacks. Can't believe how long they've been together already. I'm looking forward to seeing Ollie again, and meeting Cade too. Who knows, we could be double dating in no time xxx

Panic shot through me once again. I had no good reason for not having told Ollie about me and Noah yet. I knew when I told him he'd be over the moon for me. I mean, sure, he'd crack a lot of terrible jokes and probably give poor Noah the protective best friend speech. So why did telling him feel like such a big deal? After all, I wanted Hannah to know I had a boyfriend so she could stop messaging asking if I was okay and if I'd done any research on asexuality yet.

It just seemed that when it came to telling Ollie, I had a massive mental block. I was sure it would pass soon enough, but for now, I kind of wanted to keep Noah to myself a little bit longer.

> Haha yeah, maybe one day! xx

And just like that, New Year's Eve went from being the most exciting night of the year in my mind, to being just another source of anxiety.

There was no doubt about it, Cade knew how to stage an event. And that was just what the New Year's Eve party had turned into on his watch. No pound shop decorations and tacky streamers for him. The place looked like something out of a Hallmark movie on speed. Everything you could lay your hands on sparkled, including the man himself. He was a wonder.

"Oh my God, Cade! This place looks *incredible.* I'd ask how you did it but I'm afraid it would spoil the magic."

Beaming, he spun on the spot in a perfect pirouette before depositing a kiss on my cheek and singing, "You're welcome."

"Cheers, Lolz," Ollie huffed playfully. "Like his ego isn't already big enough."

Moving onto Ollie, Cade dropped a rather more lingering kiss on his lips that was so searing that I almost felt it was indecent to watch. "You love my big... ego."

"You two make me sick," I joked, pulling a face at their sickening affection for one another.

"Good." Ollie grinned then peered over my shoulder to where guests were starting to arrive for the New Year's Eve shenanigans. "Who's this?"

My stomach twisted and dropped when I turned and saw Noah walking purposefully towards me, smiling widely. I rushed over to him, leaving Ollie behind and hoping he'd stay there.

No such luck.

"Hey," I said, aiming for an affectionate tone but missing and landing right on panicked. "Ollie, you remember Noah? One of the old Sandy crew."

"Oh sure, hey, Noah. You're the surfer, right?" Ollie replied, his eyes scanning between the two of us curiously as we stood side by side.

Feeling Noah reaching easily for my hand, I faked a coughing fit, hoping it didn't look and sound as fake as it felt, but somehow, urgently unready for Ollie to know about our relationship. Noah instantly looked confused and a little hurt, but he schooled his features quickly into a smooth smile that only a kid whose home life was a nightmare and wanted to hide it could have pulled off. He was an open book when he was happy, but he was a master of hiding how he felt when the chips were down. It was clear; that one small gesture of pulling my hand away had hurt him more than I could ever have imagined it would.

He covered it nicely enough for the untrained eye, though, engaging Ollie in talk of surfing, Cornwall, and a fish and chip shop in Newquay they apparently both loved. I stood between them, fidgeting and awkward, wishing I could disappear through a hole in the ground but not really sure why. After all, it wasn't like I had anything to hide by dating Noah. It didn't make sense to me that I felt this way, so how on Earth was I going to explain it to Noah?

I needed to work it out and fast. His expression told me that the moment we were alone together, he was going to want answers. Answers I had no idea how to give.

Once Ollie and Noah were done sharing enthusiastic memories of Cornwall, Ollie pecked a gentle kiss to my cheek before sashaying off with Cade, promising to catch up again later on in the party. Suddenly, despite being surrounded by people, Noah and I were alone, and I could do nothing but chew on my fingernails awkwardly while looking around at all the people enjoying the party.

"Ollie doesn't know about us, does he?" Noah asked quietly after a long, torturous moment of silence.

"He, uh… no, not exactly."

"Do I want to know why?" He didn't sound angry, more hurt, and that was a million times worse.

"I don't know, okay? I don't know why. I'm just not ready for him to know yet. I want to keep us for ourselves for a bit longer. Is that so terrible?"

"You're…" He paused, inhaling deeply and letting it go before continuing. "You're ashamed of me?"

"No. Never. That's not it at all. You don't understand."

"Well, you're not exactly explaining it much."

"Because I can't. I just…" I sighed, scrubbing at my face with hands that wouldn't stop shaking. Claustrophobia strangled my voice off and I felt trapped and hounded. Despite knowing that he was entirely justified in his questions, I wanted nothing more than to get away and hide. Not quite the New Year's Eve of dreams I'd envisioned when we'd planned to spend it together.

"Oh my god, Lola!" An unexpected voice cut through the air, and the next moment I was assaulted by a whirlwind of blonde hair and arms that pulled me into a strong, warm hug.

"Hannah?" I questioned quietly in confusion.

"The very same." I could hear the smile in her voice and allowed myself to melt a little further into her hug. "I didn't know you were coming tonight. How *are* you?"

"Umm..." I started, unsure what to say to even begin to answer that question with Noah looking on in hurt and confusion.

"I'll let you two talk," he muttered, his hands dropping into his pockets as he sloped off towards the bar area, his shoulders slumped and his posture screaming unhappiness.

"Wow!" Hannah exclaimed, watching after him. "What did you do to the poor guy? Break his heart?"

I attempted a laugh but it came out more like a strangled cry that sent Hannah's eyebrows creeping up her forehead in curiosity.

"Oh, honey, we need drinks and we need snacks. Stat!"

Wordlessly, I followed her as she led me first to the bar and then back into the area where we'd talked at the last party.

"Sit," she ordered, pushing a drink into one of my hands and a plate of beige food into the other. "Now, tell Auntie Hannah what's going on."

Staring down into the clear liquid, I tried to clear my thoughts enough to make sense of how the evening had gone so wrong, and in the end, it all came down to one thing.

"What's going on is that I'm a massive idiot and I'm making a mess of everything as usual."

"Whoa, steady on there. If I'd known we were throwing a pity party I'd have brought balloons." She grinned, clearly joking, but she was right. I had no right to sit there feeling sorry for myself. It was Noah who was suffering because I couldn't just exist in a normal relationship without making a hash up of it.

Groaning loudly, I let my face fall dramatically into my

hands and forced myself not to scrub at my eyes where, for a change, I'd actually worn some make up.

"Okay, new tactic," Hannah said, refusing to give up on this conversation. "Why don't you tell me who that sad, defeated guy was who walked off just before?"

Sad and defeated. Because of me.

"That was Noah."

"Uh huh. And he was so sad because what? God didn't like his ark?"

The corner of my mouth lifted at that and I started to wonder if there was ever anything that Hannah couldn't make better.

"Because I haven't told Ollie about us yet."

"Ah," she replied with an understanding nod while drawing out the vowel sound for what felt like forever. "You're part of an 'us' now?"

"Well, I certainly was. Sad and defeated might be a deal breaker for him."

"Nah," she trilled, waving her hand dismissively. "Boys pretend they're above drama but they secretly love all of that moody stuff."

"I hope so," I huffed through a humourless laugh.

"Am I allowed to ask why you haven't told Ollie?"

I shrugged. "I just... haven't."

Her eyebrows crept up impossibly higher, and I thought I saw the hint of a smirk touch her lips before instantly disappearing.

"Well I *know* you're not protecting Ollie. I know he's had his hard times but you only have to look at him to see that these days, he's happier than a seagull in an unmanned chippy."

"No, he doesn't need protecting anymore. He's flying."

Hannah hummed in agreement, her head tilting to one side as she considered me carefully. "Are you happy with him? Noah, I mean."

"Of course. Noah's wonderful."

"I'm sure he is." She smiled. "But that's not what I asked. You know how many Prince Charmings I dated before realising that, as perfect as some of them might have been, we were never going to fit because they just weren't what my heart was looking for."

"No, it's not that. I love being with Noah. I feel… different when I'm with him. More content. Like my heart settles when he's near."

She looked surprised at how emphatic my feelings were for Noah, and maybe the words spilling from my mouth surprised me a little, too. But as I spoke them, I knew that they were the absolute truth. Noah was safety and warmth. He was tight hugs and skin tingling kisses. He was rapidly becoming the place that felt the most like home to me in the world. So how could I bear to upset him when it was something so easily fixed?

"I need to go," I announced abruptly, jumping up and knowing exactly what I needed to do. "Thank you. You always seem to be rescuing me when I'm being an idiot."

She grinned, lifting her drink to me like a toast. "Just think of me as your crazy lesbian fairy godmother. See you later, Lola. Go get him."

CHAPTER 20
NOAH

My last conversation with Lola had felt like a huge blow to my stomach. I could see her struggling to find the words I so desperately needed to hear from her.

You're right, Noah. I can tell Ollie no problem. I don't have anything to hide.

But nothing. Instead, I could practically hear the sigh of relief as a girl who seemed to know Lola came over.

I took that as my cue to walk away, because I couldn't hide the disappointment that was painted across my face, nor did I want to be known to Lola's friends or the rest of our classmates as Noah: the lad who nearly cried on New Year's Eve.

I walked over to the bar, the only place at the party where I'd be able to crutch my self-esteem after it had taken a sudden kick to the floor.

I poured everything and anything that had the highest alcohol content into a glass then propped myself up against the bar and observed the party, alone. No Sam to keep me company. No one.

Lola had disappeared off with her friend, and even though my chest ached and my heart tried to pump a little quicker through my sadness, I still found myself looking for her in the crowds.

Instead of finding her, my eyes darted to each and every couple standing, talking, dancing and even kissing, and there I was—heartbroken and alone.

I watched Alfie talking to Summer underneath a sparkling disco ball, sipping my drink through gritted teeth as the warmth burnt the back of my throat.

The last time they'd been together at a party it had ended in tears, but their conversation this time seemed more civil. Summer was smiling, laughing even, which was a rare and welcome sight around Alfie.

That boy would do or say anything to get laid.

My attention then turned to Ollie and Cade, who were singing at the top of their lungs. They seemed so content in each other's company, I couldn't help but be infected by the happiness radiating from them.

I choked back the rest of the liquor in my glass, pulled up my big boy pants, and with the help of Dutch courage, I ambled over to them.

"Hey," I yelled over the music. They both smiled and Cade gave a little wave, but they continued bellowing whatever the latest hit was that played from the speaker.

I stood awkwardly next to them, trying my best to dance along with them without looking like a third wheel, but I knew I stood out like a sore thumb.

I had to think of something, and fast.

"You both go to Allerton, don't you?" I said in a last

ditch attempt to create conversation. "My brother works there."

Cade's attention was pulled away from the music in intrigue. "Who's your brother?"

"Nate Larson. He teaches maths."

"Your brother is the hot new maths teacher? He's like the only good thing about the subject."

Ollie looked at Cade for a short second before nodding in agreement that my brother was hot.

"I wouldn't say he was hot, but yeah. He's even dating another teacher at the school."

I now had the attention of both of them. It didn't matter that the next big hit was playing from the speakers.

"Her name is Emma. She's an English teacher, I seem to remember."

That was it. Cade's mouth opened wide in shock and Ollie locked eyes with him.

"Not Miss Bennett?" they both asked in sync.

"This is major gossip. I mean, Miss Bennett and I go way back. She's an absolute babe." Cade pulled out his phone and frantically tapped away at the screen, no doubt announcing in all his group chats that Emma and my brother were in a relationship. Telling Ollie and Cade might not have been my smartest move, and I knew it was likely to bite me on the arse at some point in the near future, but for a brief moment and under the influence of alcohol, I smiled through the pain of the evening's rejection.

"Here comes trouble," Ollie said with a nod, pointing to Lola, who was walking over to us with purpose. Her expression was serious, right up until her lips crashed against mine and her eyes softened. I stood there shocked, immobilised by a kiss I hadn't expected but wholeheartedly needed. It was as though she'd bottled up all of her passion and poured it over us as our lips collided with affection.

That kiss had everything I'd ever needed from Lola. It had everything her other kisses had given me and a whole lot more.

It gave me the reassurance I needed that we were an item. We weren't in some sort of childish playground relationship. It was real. Kissing me in front of Ollie would have been a big enough deal for Lola, but as the crowds of people around us started to cheer and wolf whistle, I couldn't help but smile underneath her warm kiss.

"That's a tenner you owe me," Cade sang loudly to Ollie, cutting through the moment in his usual style.

Lola's lips slipped from mine but her head stayed pressed to my chest as she turned to glower at her best friend.

"You're taking bets on my love life now, Oliver Martin? Some friend you are."

"Well, you didn't tell me so I'm left out in the cold, forced to guess," he said, laughing openly.

"And extorting him out of his money is my only joy in life," Cade added with a wink.

"I hate you both," Lola said, not sounding as though she meant a single word of it.

I laughed at the banter between them all while soaking up as much Lola as I could before we'd be forced to mingle with everyone at the party. "Now, now, Little-Legs, cut the guys some slack. Besides, I wouldn't mind getting in on the gambling. Double or nothing, I bet Alfie and Summer are sucking faces by the end of the night."

"I seem to remember they have a very love-hate relationship, so..." Ollie said, but before he could finish speaking, Cade jumped in and shook my hand.

"You're on. I'm feeling lucky tonight."

Cade wasn't the only one feeling lucky that night. After Lola had announced our relationship to the entire party, the news of which would no doubt be spread across Allerton and Sandford before we stepped foot back through the sixth form gates, I felt invincible.

Maybe the alcohol had something to do with that, too.

I danced with Lola in my arms and even managed to sing a couple of songs I knew the words to.

The evening vanished before us through the laughs and shots that Cade made us drink—not that we took much convincing.

Before I knew it, we began counting down from ten to midnight, huddled together in Cade's back garden, if you could call it that, ready to see in the New Year.

We all raised our drinks in the air as the whistling sounds of fireworks and loud bangs sounded over our cheers as the clock struck midnight

"Happy New Year, Little-Legs."

"Happy New Year, Shark Boy," Lola said, then stood on her tiptoes to kiss me underneath the colourful glow of the fireworks.

I was so happy my heart could have exploded with joy right there, and would have lit up the sky with a thousand colours all thanks to her.

So, it turned out that Cade's famously good parties did live up to the hype. Not just for Lola and me, but for Ollie and Cade who spent the rest of the evening drinking each other's saliva, and even for Alfie and Summer.

There they were, kissing against a fence panel with Alfie pressing every inch of his body against hers. They were doing what could have only been described as sucking each other's faces, so I took a few seconds to gloat and managed to split Ollie and Cade up long enough to tell them I'd won the bet.

It had been a great party. I'd drunk more than my body could sensibly handle, I'd gambled some money and won, and I'd even arranged to spend the whole of New Years Day with my girlfriend.

"Not another movie about the dangers of open water, please?" I pleaded with Lola, hoping that we'd spend our first ever New Years Day together doing some other activity like going for a walk or testing her baking skills in the kitchen rather than watching another shark attack film on her couch. Of course, Lola had other plans.

"I'm not going to rest until you accept that there is a chance you could be eaten by a shark. I don't want my boyfriend being mauled by a vicious sea predator."

"For a start, sharks aren't vicious. They just get scared when they see us, weirdly-shaped-humans, flailing about in the water. Secondly, I've decided that my New Year's Resolution this year is to not only get you over your unwarranted fear of being attacked by sea creatures, but it's also to try to teach you to surf." I smiled and watched her expression turn to a look of horror.

"I know that traditionally, New Year's resolutions are doomed to failure, but you're really knocking the likelihood of success down to rock bottom with that one." She chuckled and patted my chest with her hand playfully.

"Oh yeah? Well, I'm on a winning streak with Alfie and Summer kissing, so I'd bet a whole lot right now on me getting you surfing. You might even like it. Besides, I think you'd look pretty hot in a wetsuit."

"Such a shame to throw away a winning streak like that." She tutted loudly and shook her head.

"You really do lack confidence in me. I'm even more determined to make this happen now. I'll even sweeten the deal and treat you to a couple of nights away in a cottage near the sea so we don't have to stay in a tent or my brother's camper. I can make it all romantic and stuff. How about now?" I opened my eyes widely and fluttered my eyelashes just a little, wearing the biggest puppy dog eyes I could. I looked at her like Dave looked at me when I was holding a fresh cut of salmon for him.

"You want to take me away to stay in a lovely cottage by the sea, go nuts," she said, grinning. "But the surfing thing? Not happening. Never. Never, ever, ever. This girl doesn't go in the ocean. Give it up, Shark Boy. It's never going to happen!"

CHAPTER 21
LOLA

How was this happening?

I'd always considered myself a stubborn person. All of my life, I'd dug my heels in over the most petty things, even refusing to eat breakfast cereal that wasn't the right brand. My stubbornness was so deeply entrenched in my personality at that point that I was just short of listing it as a special skill on my university applications.

So, how was it that I found myself, four months after swearing it would never, ever happen, standing on a windy Cornish beach wearing a wetsuit and ready to cringe, flinch and grumble my way through surfing lessons with Noah and his brother?

As I'd always assumed, I looked like a demented penguin in the stupid wetsuit, and despite only having paddled in the shallows, where foamy white waves lapped the shore, I'd already screamed twice at something (clearly a monster of the deep) touching my feet.

Of course, Noah looked effortlessly perfect, like something out of Home and Away. This was his kingdom—the place he was the most at home. With sand between his toes and the sunlight glinting off his blond curls, he was every bit the Cornish surfer dude.

I'd seen girls on the beach, in their skimpy bikinis with gorgeous beachy waves in their hair, eyeing him up with interest. To say I wanted to scratch their eyes right out wouldn't have been an exaggeration at all.

Here, he was king, and I felt like an unworthy peasant beside him as he laughed at my disgust at the entire ocean and its contents.

"You do know that fish wee in there, don't you, Shark Boy?" I demanded when he tugged lightly on my hand, trying to move me past the shoreline and into the shark-infested part.

"True, but that's like one percent of the ocean's contents. The other ninety-nine percent is delicious sea water just ready and waiting to swim in. Anyway, the first lesson is how to get on the board, and well, if you're any good at the surfing part, you won't be spending much time in the water."

"Ugh," I huffed, eyeing the unwieldy board with distaste. They always looked so slick and manageable when you saw people running down the beach with them in films. In real life, it was bigger than me and I was absolutely convinced it was going to cause my death. "If I get eaten by a shark or die of some awful water-borne disease, I'm coming back as a ghost just to haunt you when you're trying to sleep."

Noah chuckled a little while ushering me into the water. "And if that happens, I'll accept it wholeheartedly, but it won't. Trust me."

"Pfft. There is no trust here—just deep loathing and a strong hope you at least come away from this weekend with sunburn."

My toes curled at the unnatural way the water tickled around them, and I clung onto Noah for dear life.

A quick glance over his shoulder showed me the vision of Nate and his girlfriend, Emma, also a novice, spending more time enjoying each other in the water than doing anything that could remotely be described as surfing.

Did she actually enjoy having his hands all over her body like that? Or was she just distracting him from the lesson any way she knew how?

I stared as his hands roamed to places I was surprised to see them go in public, but Emma looked positively gleeful about it.

Noah glanced over his shoulder, following my gaze, pulled a face, and returned his eyes to mine.

"Okay, teach me, oh wise Shark Boy," I quipped, trying to hide the way my entire body wanted to curl away from what was happening over his shoulder.

"As you wish, Little-Legs. Okay, so I'm going to stand behind you in the water, and I'll help you get on the board." Noah's hands landed on my hips as we waded ourselves deeper into the water. The sun was shining but the water was still freezing cold.

"Something just touched my foot!" I screamed, convinced the Creature from the Black Lagoon was coming to drag me into the murky green depths.

"Well, get on the board and you'll be safe from the monsters lurking beneath the waves." I could practically hear Noah rolling his eyes.

"Just so you know, I spoke to Satan last night and he's

preparing a really special seat for you in Hell. Right by the fire," I grumbled, gasping as a wave hit me full force in the face and salt water flew up my nose and down my throat. "I can't believe you do this for fun," I continued to mutter, almost inaudibly, as I attempted, fruitlessly, to throw my body onto the surfboard as it bobbed merrily on the waves around us.

"It is fun, and although we're not doing much surfing, I'm having fun with you. It's fun to watch you thoroughly hate every second of this." Noah smirked as another wave crashed into us.

"Some bloody Prince Charming you're turning out to be," I protested as he gripped my hips and helped me to jump onto the top of the board, where I perched precariously, waiting for death to take me.

"That's it. You're on the board. You're going to be a pro in no time. Now, let's try your balance. Try to stand up." Before I could open my mouth to question his sanity, he continued. "I've got you. You'll be fine."

"I hate you so much, Noah Larson," I yelled for the whole of Cornwall to hear, clinging onto the board for dear life as I attempted to push to my knees.

Predictably, the whole thing flipped over and I landed face first in the water.

Splashing like a toddler, I found my way back to the surface and gasped, coughing to clear the godforsaken fish-wee-water from my mouth and lungs.

Then, turning on Noah, who was watching and laughing, I narrowed my eyes and growled, "Are we having fun yet?"

"Honestly. Surfing has never, ever been this fun before." Laughter escaped Noah uncontrollably. Not even my glare could stop him. A few minutes in and once he'd calmed down, he swiped his finger across my forehead to tame the dripping hair that swept my face, as well as picking out some seaweed that had clung to my hair.

"I hope Lego plagues every barefoot step you take for the rest of your life," I hissed, swiping my hand through the water and splashing him. Of course, the splash did absolutely nothing to destroy his mood or how natural he looked in this environment. If I hadn't hated it so much, I might have taken a moment to enjoy the sight of him in his happy place. As it was, I just wanted to get out of there before something with more teeth than compassion got hold of me and I died a watery and unpleasant death. "Is it dry land time yet? The sun cream you insisted I wore has now run into my eyes and I can see at least three of you."

"Fine, it's dry land time, but only for today. I'm definitely getting you back on this board before our holiday is out, no excuses." Noah gave me a gentle kiss before shouting over to his brother. "Yo, Nate. Fancy showing these ladies how it's done?"

Relieved, I let him take my hand and lead me to the sand, effortlessly carrying the board with the other hand like it weighed nothing. I could have kissed the land as I fell to my knees and thanked it loudly for existing.

"You ain't getting me back in that water until I find some sunglasses," I demanded, squinting through the stinging of my eyes as the sunscreen launched its assault.

"I'll tell you what, once I've hit the waves for a bit, I'll treat you to a brand new pair. It looks like Emma's coming to join you anyhow."

"Ah, thank goodness. Sanity!" I flipped sand at him as he dropped a sweet kiss on my salty cheek before running off to join his brother in the water. Emma flopped down on the sand beside me and we watched as they paddled their boards way out beyond the waves and then hopped up on top like spring gazelles, catching waves to the shore as though it were nothing.

"It's so hot when he does that," Emma said, practically drooling at the sight of Nate mastering the waves like he was Poseidon.

I huffed a non committal sound in response, and the two of us sat and watched them tame the ocean over and over, sometimes silent and sometimes sympathising with each other over how much we were never going to enjoy surfing.

The sun shifted slowly across the sky and, with my feet firmly on dry land, I found myself much more able to admire Noah's long, agile form as he bent and curled in tune with every movement of every wave he rode to the shore.

As the sun moved slowly into my eye line, destroying my view of the show the boys were putting on for us, I decided the sunglasses couldn't wait any longer.

At the top of the beach, beside the car park where Nate's car was sitting, there was a small ice cream shack slash gift shop and I could see the rotating racks of cheap, tacky sunglasses standing outside from the beach.

By the time I reached the shop, my eyes were stinging a little less, but my discomfort in the wetsuit, which hid precisely none of my curves, was real.

The self consciousness I felt was only compounded when I was confronted by that same group of stunningly beautiful beachy girls, all gathered around the front of the shop buying drinks and chatting loudly. About my boyfriend.

Nothing deflated a girl's self esteem more than a gang of beautiful girls talking about how much they'd like to sleep with your boyfriend. In graphic detail.

With shaking hands, I grabbed the first pair of sunglasses my fingers found and stumbled awkwardly past the girls, who giggled at my ineptitude. I slammed the glasses down on the counter, stammering out an order for drinks and thrusting cash at the person serving me.

Without waiting for change, I fled, sand flying up behind me as I ran across the beach to where Emma was sitting, still contentedly watching the boys in the water while playing games on her phone.

"Whoa, you okay?" she asked in surprise when I skidded to a stop beside her and thrust a bottle of water at her.

"Yeah," I replied unconvincingly, forcing the bright red sunglasses I was fairly sure were meant to be for children onto my face so she couldn't see the tears stinging at my eyes.

Noah could have any girl he wanted. So why was he with me?

"Yeah, try again, and make it believable this time, sweetie," Emma said kindly, patting the sand beside her in offering.

"Ugh," I sighed, flopping down onto the spot she'd gestured to. "I just hate the way I feel when I'm around girls who are beautiful and know it."

Emma peered over her shoulder in the direction of the shop, stared for a moment and then her mouth formed an "oh" of understanding.

"Oh, honey, you do not need to worry about those girls. Have you seen the way Noah looks at you? I swear to god I haven't seen a lad that smitten since I played matchmaker for Ollie and Cade!"

I gaped at her for a moment, until I realised I probably resembled a goldfish with my month opening and closing wordlessly. "Wait. You're *the* English teacher?"

She grinned. "The very same."

"Oh my god! You're the stuff of legend. Ollie talks about you all the time. Did you really dress up as Macbeth on World Book Day then spend the entire day sending threatening messages to the person dressed as Banquo?"

"Maybe." She smirked. "All's fair in love and war, and all that."

"Incredible. You're a minor celebrity on TikTok after that, you know?"

"Well, it doesn't hurt to be cool in the eyes of the students." She laughed and lay back in the sand, resting on her elbows.

Silence descended over us once again, leaving me to stew in my mind over every one of my insecurities.

It wasn't like I was a hideous monster. But some girls just had that thing, that magic that made them cooler than everybody else. Whatever that was, I did not have it.

Did it matter to Noah?

Did he look at those girls and then at me and wonder what on earth he was doing?

Lost in my ever spiralling thoughts, I cheated myself out of what remained of the surf show Noah and Nate were putting on for us. I didn't snap back into reality until I felt a wet, sandy hand caressing my cheek and tasted salt as Noah's lips kissed mine gently.

"Have you recovered from your trauma?" he asked playfully.

"That one's gonna linger to be honest," I joked in return. "I'm gonna need dessert tonight to even begin to get over the pain and suffering."

He grinned, holding out his hand to me and pulling me to my feet when I placed mine in it. "Good job I have dinner plans for us then, isn't it?"

CHAPTER 22
NOAH

Surfing with Nate was always fun——no matter the season or the amount of eyes glued to the way we rode our boards and how they flicked water into the air. Everyone ashore was looking, but the only eyes I cared about were Lola's. I actively sought her out all while doing my best to not embarrass myself.

Once I was back on dry land, my feet churned up the sandy beach running to Lola and Emma, who were now sitting at the top of the beach near some rocks. I didn't tell Lola that they were the very rocks I'd slipped on only a few months before and ended up with my arm in a cast.

Thankfully, I'd escaped with no broken bones or rocky accidents this time, and I even had Lola around to kiss any minor injuries better. I almost considered faking a shark attack to prompt another kiss from her.

But rather than getting all shy and waiting for her to initiate a kiss, I placed my lips against hers and felt hers respond readily. They moved together so perfectly, it was like they'd spent a month in rehearsals. I didn't even care that Emma was sitting right next to Lola, because no doubt my brother would be groping her in no time.

I listened to Lola ranting about how traumatic her attempt at surfing had been, if you could call it that. I suspected it was all a ploy to get dessert. My girl would do anything for sugary treats, so it was pretty lucky that I'd planned her favourite for that evening.

I'd saved up a couple of weeks of my allowance, and even borrowed some money from Nate, just to make sure I had enough to treat her the way she deserved to be treated.

It was worth the debt, as Lola's eyes widened in awe as we approached our lighthouse style cottage. Its white and red stripes looked like they'd had been recently repainted, bringing the disused lighthouse back to life.

"It's amazing, isn't it?" I said, reaching for Lola's hand.

She turned her face to me, beaming with a bright smile and cheeks pink from the sun. "It's perfect," she whispered, curling her fingers between mine.

"I'm just sorry we have to share it with my brother and his girlfriend."

She shrugged like it was irrelevant to her. "They're nice. I really like your brother. He's a lot like you. And his girlfriend is responsible for Ollie and Cade getting together. Did you know that?"

"I don't know whether me being a lot like my brother is a good thing." I laughed and nudged her playfully. "Oh, yeah. I may have been the one who told Ollie and Cade at the New Year's Eve party. I still don't think Nate has forgiven me for how quickly that spread around his workplace."

"Yeah, Ollie and Cade have many talents. Party staging

is one. Gossip is another. It's practically a special skill at this point."

"Well, speaking of special skills, I'm hoping to prove myself even more to you tonight." I looked smugly at her, as excited as a dog gets the minute you say walkies just to see her beaming smile. It was that smile that filled me with so much warmth, I could spend every day in the freezing cold as long as I had her in my heart.

"You mean using me as shark bait earlier wasn't the high point of the trip? Why, Mr Shark Boy, you spoil me." She grinned and nudged my shoulder playfully.

"It was a high point for me," I said through laughter. "But I knew I was going to have to sweeten the deal somehow. Besides, we've been together for over four months now, so I had to do something to celebrate our fourth-monthsary together."

"Aww look at you all making up words just to be cute," she teased, pecking a light kiss on my cheek. She smelled like sea water, fresh air and sun cream—three of my favourite smells in the world.

"It's a real word, I'll have you know. Google says so."

We walked through into the lounge, dumped our beach kit and made our way up to our room with our cases so we could get showered and changed. What Lola was oblivious to, was that Nate and Emma were secretly in the room at the top of the lighthouse, preparing it for our date. The lantern room still had most of its original features, but even that wasn't as special as it could be for her.

Lola took a shower first and emerged from the en-suite with just a large white towel wrapped around her.

"Have you seen how burnt I am?" Lola pointed to bright pink patches on her arms and face.

"You look like a drumstick lolly." I laughed and took cover for the inevitable. Her choice of weapon was a pillow from the bed, which she slammed against me a few times while giggling.

"This is why I don't go outside, Shark Boy. Fresh air is for stupid people who enjoy pain."

"God, you sound like Sam going on about his constant need to be inside playing video games. The fresh air does you good. Don't you feel invigorated right now?"

"I feel like it doesn't matter how much I shower, I'm still going to be finding sand in… places for weeks. I'm not sure that's the textbook definition of invigorated." She sounded so serious; it was only her playful grin that told me she was messing with me.

"Well, put your feet up and relax. It's all going to be worthwhile, I promise. I'm going to go for a shower now and get ready. All will be revealed soon."

I stood underneath the rain shower head, images of Lola filling my mind. My brain was so full I could barely think about anything else, and the images of her were so vivid, my senses came alive. The way her hair became wavy when it was wet… I could practically smell her. I could almost feel her soft, moisturised skin against me. I could even feel her kiss.

With every new image of Lola, my heart raced. It felt so intense, it was like it was jumping out of my skin trying its best to get to Lola in the other room.

I'd never felt like this about anyone before.

I wouldn't ever feel this way about anyone else again, and that was okay. Lola was the one. She always had been.

I buried my face into a towel and ruffled my hair, drying it into a mess of curls and waves, brushed my teeth and pulled on a change of clothes ready for that evening.

Lola had already changed out of the towel into a purple summer dress. It was likely the most colour I'd ever seen her wear, and she looked as beautiful as ever.

"Woah. You look… wow."

She flushed and dipped her head down to look at her feet. "Uh, thanks," she muttered, obviously embarrassed. "So do you."

I looked down at my pale blue shirt and mustard coloured chino pants, rubbing down my shirt a couple of times. "Thought I'd try to make an effort. Are you ready?"

Dipping a curtsy as though we were characters in a regency novel, she smiled demurely and said, "Lead the way, kind sir."

We walked from our room into the lounge, where Nate and Emma were waiting with a basket of goodies I'd had them prepare, including our very own afternoon tea and a bottle of Prosecco.

"Don't you two look the cutest couple," my brother teased with a wit-woo. I gave him a stern look before Emma ordered us to stand next to each other so she could take a picture on her polaroid camera.

I didn't know if it was nerves or excitement, but my body trembled as we stood next to each other. My arm sat at the top of Lola's back but every few seconds, it slid further down until it sat at the bottom of her back and I felt her tense.

We both smiled for the flash of the camera, even having another picture of Lola kissing my cheek, standing on her tip-toes at the request of my brother.

"Have you quite finished?" I asked him, straight faced.

His only response was a smirk. He best have done a good job. I hoped Emma would have made sure of that being the romantic she clearly was.

"Enjoy, you two," Emma said softly.

"Yeah, enjoy, love birds," Nate teased once more before I led Lola up the long spiral staircase to the lantern room.

I looked back at her as we made it to the top. Her eyes sparkled, reflecting the flickering of a thousand fairy lights hung on the metal railings. Tea lights had been lit and placed strategically to create a pathway to a blanket placed on the floor covered in multicoloured rose petals.

As she took it all in, her lips quivered up into the most beautiful smile, and she breathed, "Wow, it looks so pretty. You did all this for me?"

"Yup. It seemed like the perfect place for a date, especially because… well, you make all of my dark days bright again." I watched her expression soften as she took a step closer to me. Her arms wrapped tightly around me and she pressed her lips gently against mine. Her breath intertwined with mine and, in that moment, Lola's kiss made me feel as bright as a caffeine addict after their first coffee. She lit me up brighter than the lighthouse could ever light up the waves of the ocean at night.

"It's perfect," she whispered into my ear, her warm breath fanning over my skin. "I don't know what I did to deserve you."

"You did nothing other than being you, and that's all I'll ever need."

We sat down on the blanket and I opened up the wicker basket filled to the brim with savoury and sweet treats, along with a bottle of fizz and plastic flutes.

We tucked into the food excitedly. There was nothing

like a day out on the waves to give you an appetite. Conversation and jokes flowed easily as we ate and enjoyed. And then we came to the most important food of the night, famous in Cornwall, and apparently also Lola's favourite.

"So, the real question is, cream or jam first?" I asked as I pulled out the scones with the fresh clotted cream and strawberry jam and placed them on the blanket.

Her eyes lit up at the sight of them and I knew instantly that the cream tea idea was a win. "Well, I'm not a maniac, so obviously I put the jam on first. Only dangerously insane people go cream first, right?" She tilted her head at me, grinning widely.

"The Cornish people will be jumping with glee right now, but I actually prefer it the Devon way. The cream acts as the butter. You can't get nearly enough cream on it if you put the jam on first. It slides off and doesn't stick properly. I will admit, I do feel a bit like a traitor to be in Cornwall and blaspheming like this."

She feigned shock, throwing her hand to her chest and gaping at me in horror. "Oh my god. I'm dating a sociopath. I always knew there was something not right about you, Noah Larson, and now I know what it is."

"Don't all the best love stories involve a mix of conventional and unconventional? Like Beauty and the Beast, and Lady and the Tramp. It would be boring if we were both normal, both the same, wouldn't it?" I popped open the bottle of Prosecco and poured, trying not to let the bubbles spill over the rim of the glass.

"So, what you're saying is that I should be glad you don't have a tail?" she asked through laughter that made the air even lighter.

"Exactly. And what you lack in cookery skills you make up for in your obscene aversion to the water. Cheers to us."

We clinked our plastic glasses together and I looked into Lola's eyes as I drank. She was my beacon of light, my favourite part of each day and the reason I looked forward to the next.

Maybe it was time our relationship was clicked up a notch.

Maybe, just maybe, tonight would be my lucky night.

CHAPTER 23
LOLA

Everything was perfect. The lighthouse, the food, the boy—all of it. I'd never dreamed of having a night like this with someone I really liked. It was all wonderful, even down to the fairy lights twinkling around us and the fizz of the Prosecco that bubbled in my stomach, joining with the butterflies that Noah Larson always seemed to set loose in there.

The way he'd looked at me all evening felt different somehow. There was an intensity there that hadn't been there before, and it mingled with the butterflies in my stomach, leaving me somehow elated and nervous all at once.

Once we were full, we stepped out onto the balcony at the top of the lighthouse together, and the view of the ocean in the darkness, reflecting the moonlight, stole my breath. It felt like there was magic hanging in the air, and my chest filled with an unnamed emotion that had me flying into Noah's arms and kissing him in the moonlight until our lips were numb and our skin was cool with the evening chill.

"Shall we go down?" Noah asked, his voice a little cautious but filled with promise and hope.

"Yeah. Yes," I croaked, accepting the hand he offered me and following him back inside and down the winding stairs.

Inside, Nate and Emma were long gone, presumably to their bedroom. The air hung heavy with expectation, and I swallowed down a gulp of anxiety at the implications, forcing myself to follow him into the bedroom where there were more rose petals scattered across the covers, and candles burning on every available surface.

"Oh," I gasped, staring at the room while Noah stood beside me, unsure what to do or what to say.

"Surprise."

He wasn't kidding. My stomach clenched as his hand landed on the small of my back and he pulled me into him for another searing kiss. This time, though, I could feel the magic starting to drain away, leaving a strange feeling behind that I couldn't quite put my finger on.

Still, this was Noah, the boy I was one hundred percent head over heels for. There was no danger here, nothing to make my head swim and my insides twist like this.

Hands and arms were everywhere as he guided us gently onto the bed, scattering those blood red petals all over the place. Robotically, I kissed him back, but the usual warmth I felt at his kisses had been replaced by an icy cold feeling.

His hands began to explore my body, slowly working their way under my dress and working it lovingly up my skin, which pebbled with goosebumps. His whispered oaths about how beautiful I was, how perfect, how I made him feel, all fell on deaf ears that were filled with the sound of my own blood racing through my veins.

And then his fingers grazed lightly over my chest and my blood turned to concrete inside me, my entire body frozen in place.

I couldn't move, couldn't breathe.

Everything that had been so perfect suddenly turned to ash around me, and panic left me paralysed there on the bed with the boy I wanted more than anything to be able to love like a normal girl would.

Sensing the change in me, he paused his explorations, lifting himself up on his arms and gazing into my eyes in concern.

"Are you alright? You seem… I dunno. Am I doing this wrong?"

The concern in his eyes broke me in two, and I couldn't stop the tears from flooding my eyes. The concrete in my veins turned to lava and had me yanking away from him and huddling against the headboard with my knees pulled tight against my chest.

"No. No, you're perfect. I'm…" A sob erupted from me and my hand flew to my mouth as more and more choked free. "You're perfect. It's me. I'm all wrong."

With tears streaming down my cheeks, I leaped from the bed, tugging my dress down frantically, and ran from the room as though it were on fire.

Every pulse beat pounded in my ears, each one screaming at me that I was a freak as I ran down the stairs and careered out of the front door.

A beautiful boy I was desperately in love with wanted to take our relationship to the next level. Any other girl would have been ecstatic that he wanted her in that way, so what the hell was wrong with me? Why couldn't I just… be like everybody else?

My legs carried me mindlessly down to the beach where earlier in the day, I'd been so loved up. But now… now everything was broken.

Stones and shells cut into my feet as I ran to the shoreline, but I paid them no mind. Nothing could hurt as much as the knowledge that I couldn't give Noah what he wanted. What he deserved. He'd gone out of his way to make everything about this trip perfect. He'd arranged the most amazing, romantic evening, and then I'd thrown it all back in his face by running.

I was the worst girlfriend, the worst person. I screamed my pain, my frustration and my self-hatred into the night sky, grabbing a handful of rocks and sand and hurling them into the water, as though the action could somehow fix this night that had turned from a dream to a nightmare.

I could hear hurried steps behind me, Noah's voice calling my name, but how could I turn to him? How could I ever face him again?

My arms curled tightly around my waist and I sank to my knees in the sand, wishing that the waves would creep further up the beach and wash me away with them.

"Lola! Lola… wait up." I heard his voice behind me. "What's wrong? Are you okay?"

How was I meant to answer that? Was I okay? No. Absolutely not. But how could I tell him that the reason was something deep inside myself that I'd been trying so hard to ignore, to push to one side and hope it went away?

"Please, Noah, just… I can't right now."

"I'm sorry if I did something wrong. I never wanted to

make you feel like this. Please talk to me," he begged as the moonlight lit up his worried face.

"You did nothing wrong, Noah. You're perfect. Everything was perfect. Everything except me. It's all me. I'm broken or something. You should go back inside and forget about me. Just go."

"I'm not leaving you. Look, if you aren't ready, that's okay. I can wait. Just come inside with me and we can talk."

Emotion crashed through me, every feeling I'd felt since that beautiful moment on the balcony filling me up and utterly overwhelming me to the point where all I could do was scream in his face, "I'm never going to be ready, Noah. Never. So just go back inside. Please, just leave me."

"I don't understand. Help me understand. I'll hate myself forever if something stupid like this ruins us. Please. Please, Lola." Noah huffed through tears that were caught in his throat.

"Don't hate yourself," I cried out, pushing my hands into his chest in an attempt to make him leave me. "Hate *me*. This is all me. I'm not right. I'm not built right. I can't do this. I never should have made you think I could. I never should have convinced myself I could."

"I'm sorry the timing wasn't right. I just thought... ah, I don't even know what I was thinking." Noah pulled at his hair in frustration. "I love you, Lola. Can we please forget about what hasn't happened and go inside?"

His voice was so choked and desperate it killed me to turn away from him, but I didn't have the words to explain to him what was happening. I didn't understand it myself. All I could think about were those words

Hannah had said to me what felt like a lifetime ago now.

Have you considered the possibility that you might be ace?

I'd worked so hard to prove that I wasn't. It had never occurred to me that there were some things I wouldn't be able to fake. Not until now.

"I can't do this, Noah. I'm sorry. I shouldn't have led you on all this time. You are amazing and you deserve somebody who can be completely yours. And that's not me. I'm sorry."

"What are you saying? We're in Cornwall for heaven's sake. What are we supposed to do? What can I do?"

"Just go inside. I'll get a train home tomorrow."

"It's the middle of the night. What are you going to do until then? You aren't staying out here on your own."

Tears streamed down my face as I looked at the blurred vision of him pleading with me, this boy I could never begin to deserve. Even when I was standing here breaking his heart, he was being a gentleman and worrying about my safety. I could feel all the fractured pieces of my heart stabbing at my chest as I shook my head, looking down at my feet because seeing the light of hope still burning in his eyes hurt too much.

"I'll be fine. Worry about you, the person who deserves it."

"I've spent my whole life worrying. I worry about my mum constantly. I worry I'll never live up to the man my brother has become. The one thing I never thought I'd have to worry about is you. I can't help but worry that something I love so dearly is slipping away. I need to hold on to you, Lola. I can't let you go." He paused for a second to catch his breath and clear his throat. "Please, don't let me go."

Every word he said cut a little deeper until I was broken and bleeding right in front of him, standing there without a mark on me. "I have to, Noah. You have to let me go. I never wanted to hurt you, but I can't keep pretending. I can't."

"Will you please come back with me? We can talk in the morning and... I'll even sleep on the couch. Please."

Shaking my head, my hair sticking to the tears still falling down my cheeks, I couldn't stand the thought of sleeping in that room where he'd planned the perfect night for us. Together.

"I'll take the couch," I insisted, conceding to his demand to go inside because he clearly wasn't giving up.

"Are you sure? I don't mind. I want you to be comfortable." We began the slow walk up the beach back towards the lighthouse. The closer we got, the more my stomach filled with dread.

"I'm sure."

The rest of the walk was made in a pained silence only broken by the steady ebb and flow of the waves in the background, a sound that had always soothed me in the past. Now, all I'd be able to think of when I heard it would be this moment. The scent of salt in the air would forever make the scar tissue in my chest ache.

Back inside, the warmth of the living room wrapped around me like a hug I didn't deserve. Noah stood helplessly beside me for a moment, perhaps expecting me to speak, but I had nothing to say, no words of comfort to fix what I'd broken. Eventually, he sighed, digging his hands into the pockets of his trousers, and disappeared upstairs, returning moments later with armfuls of bedding.

His eyes lingered on mine for a moment, filled with hurt, before he left again, and the house fell into silence.

I didn't sleep. How could I? My mind was filled with a million and one thoughts, images of what might have been, the pain in his words stinging me over and over as the hours ticked away. I dreaded the moment he woke and came to find me.

How was I meant to explain this to him when I didn't fully understand it myself?

In a fortunate turn of events I definitely didn't deserve, Noah was beaten to the stairs by his brother who was apparently an early riser. When he sleepily stumbled into the room and saw me sitting there wound up in the bedding, his eyes widened and instantly filled with worry.

"Lola? What are you doing down here? You okay?"

He came closer when I didn't answer, slowly taking in the tear tracks down my cheeks and my eyes, still red and sore from crying most of the night.

"You want a cuppa?" he asked after a long period of uncomfortable silence.

I shook my head, my voice eventually croaking out, "Please would you be able to drive me to the train station?"

Clearly taken aback by the request, his eyebrows shot up even higher and he cupped the back of his neck with his hand, looking torn.

"Of course I will. But... why?"

"I just... I need to go home. As soon as possible."

"Did my little brother do something to hurt you?" he asked cautiously.

"No! No. I just… I can't explain."

He considered me for the longest time before sighing and tugging at his hair in a move that reminded me sharply of his brother.

"Fine, I'll drive you on the agreement that you let me pay for your train and you let me see you onto it so I know you're safe."

I opened my mouth to protest, but his face and posture were so teacher-like that I knew it was non-negotiable. I nodded silently, and moved to use the bathroom to freshen up quickly, keen to get out of there before Noah woke up.

The car journey was awkward and silent, but for the soft music playing on Nate's radio, not loud enough to break the tension that was thickening the air between us. Outside the station, Nate sat, clutching the steering wheel. His profile was so much like Noah's that it hurt to look at him, but it was clear he was working up to speaking.

Eventually, he cleared his throat before asking quietly, "You're sure he didn't do anything to hurt you?"

"I'm sure," I said. "Thank you for the lift. And Nate?"

He lifted his chin in an invitation to go on.

"Please look after him. He'll need you today."

"Sure thing, Lola," he said softly, looking at me with eyes filled with concern and a forehead creased in worry.

"Thank you," I whispered before allowing him to escort me into the station.

CHAPTER 24
NOAH

What had I done?

In a few short seconds, my seemingly perfect relationship had crumbled into nothing. All that remained was the ache in my chest, puddles of tears and the bright red of my bloodshot eyes.

I must have dozed off at some point in the night and had the events replay as a nightmare, only waking when the current of the ocean dragged me out into the open water and further away from the love of my life.

And now, wide awake, I watched out of the window as Lola got into my brother's car, leaving me feeling even more broken, even more hopeless, because all I wanted to do was try to fix it. She wasn't letting me.

My fist smashed uncontrollably against the concrete wall of the lighthouse, leaving the wall and my brother's security deposit unscathed but my knuckles broken and bleeding.

I sucked in a breath of air at the stabbing pain, but it was nothing compared to the stinging in my chest.

"Noah, do you want pancakes?"

Normally I'd have jumped at the chance but I felt physically sick and I'd lost my appetite for food—I'd lost my appetite for anything at all.

"Nah, I'm alright." I turned and grabbed a dark navy hoodie, shoving it over me and attempting to leave, but Emma stood in my tracks.

"What have you done?" Her eyes glanced at my knuckles.

"Nothing. I just want to go." My voice rose and my frown deepened. I didn't want to be with anyone. I didn't want to be anywhere. I thought about running to the beach, but for the first time in my life, I couldn't think of a worse place to be.

"Calm down. Whatever is going on, I'm here. I've got you. Can I at least take a look at your knuckles?"

"Fine," I grunted, looking down in defeat. I didn't have the energy to argue back.

She led me into the kitchen, grabbing the travel first aid kit, then sat me down to tend to the broken skin covering my knuckles.

I hissed each time the antiseptic wipe grazed against the raw cuts as she wiped over them, cleaning up the blood that had begun to dry, but not once did I make eye contact.

"Before Nate left, he nipped into our room to let me know he was taking Lola to the train station. Is that how this happened?" she asked.

"I didn't hit her." I didn't want to speak, but I couldn't let my brother's girlfriend think that of me.

"Oh, Noah. Gosh, I didn't mean that. I know you wouldn't do that. You're so kind hearted and I know how deep your love is for her. What I meant was, are these cuts the result of a broken heart?"

I nodded. I couldn't speak—not about how much I loved her. I couldn't bear to say the words again and not have her say them back. I'd told Lola twice on the beach that I loved her, but I hadn't got the response I wanted back. I'd relived those moments so many times that they were permanently etched deep into my mind.

"I'm sorry, Noah. I don't know what's happened, but I'm here if you want to talk about it. You don't have to suffer alone."

I glanced up, my eyes meeting hers for just a second, and I tried to smile to thank her. I must have looked a mess, but I wasn't sure what else I expected—barely any sleep, girlfriend-less and wishing to be anywhere but Cornwall.

After Emma had finished cleaning up my knuckles, on her advice, I went for a walk around the block. I tried my best not to contact Lola, but it was hard when everything seemed to remind me of her: the distant sounds of complaining voices, a kid playing with an inflatable dinosaur, and a pair of red sunglasses, similar to the ones she'd worn the day before—the day our waves had crashed into a foaming mess. A lot had changed since our waters had been calm and crystal clear blue and my world had been smooth sailing.

I wasn't sure how long I walked for, but by the time I got back to the lighthouse, my stomach churned at the sight of Nate's car parked back outside.

I opened the door and was immediately met with interrogating eyes from Nate, and he started questioning me straight away.

"Are you going to tell me what's happened?" Nate said, without pleasantries and with seemingly no care for my wellbeing.

"No."

"Why not? Your girlfriend slept on the damn couch. What happened?" He pushed further, and the more he did, the more I lost my patience.

"It's none of your damn business. Now, can you leave me alone? Not really in the most Cornwall-y mood."

"Well, if you'd tell me what you've done, maybe we can stop talking about it," he continued, but this time Emma jumped in.

"Cut him some slack. He'll talk when he's ready."

"I don't even *know* what I've done. Have I done something wrong? I couldn't tell you. Lola kept telling me I haven't but that's pretty fucking hard to believe when I'm stood here, on my first ever holiday with a girlfriend, without my girlfriend." My voice carried, seeming to echo up to the lantern room of the lighthouse and out across the ocean. "She's not my girlfriend any more. She made that clear last night and cemented it this morning by not replying to my text messages... Is she safe?"

Nate's voice softened, no longer laced with an accusatory tone. "Yeah. She's on a train home. I've told her to message me when she's back so I know she's safe. I'll let you know when I hear from her again."

Nate did let me know she got home safe, and I was pleased for that at least. She was at home, safe and sound, but still not replying to my messages. There was dead silence between us, not that I'd expected any different.

Lola was home and I was in Cornwall.

With my brother and his girlfriend. I was the epitome of a third wheel, and boy did they amplify that feeling.

With all the kisses and hugs, and the general sickness-inducing actions, I spent as much time as I could in the room that brought back the worst of memories. The few remaining stray rose petals on the floor made sure I couldn't forget. But it was better than watching my sibling fawn over a woman who had set up Lola's best friend with the love of his life. Pity she didn't have any more of those Cupid arrows to fire at Lola and me.

What I'd have done to rewind.

I sat in bed, hour after hour, mindlessly scrolling and clinging onto desperation—hoping that Lola would message me back. She never did. Instead, the phone battery depleted time and time again, until we were ready to leave the beaches and pasties behind. I couldn't wait to see the back of them.

As much as I wanted to see Lola, I also knew the moment I did, I'd be confronted with further rejection I couldn't face. Not yet, anyway. Thankfully, we still had one week left of our Easter break so I didn't have to face her until going back to Sandford.

I hid away from everyone, even Mum and Dad, who were giving me a wide berth, no doubt thanks to a pre-warning from my brother.

Once again, I was alone in my room, scrolling on my phone until I couldn't look at the picture perfect worlds that everyone seemed to have plastered all over their social media accounts.

After much internal deliberation, I got up and turned on my Xbox that had been gathering dust since the last time I'd used it. Within seconds of appearing online, I received a message from Sam.

> WHAMBAMTHANKUSAM:
>
> What the hell are you doing online? Watching a DVD? Lol

> NOAH14:
>
> Do you even have a life outside of your console? What game are you on? Mind if I join you?

> WHAMBAMTHANKUSAM:
>
> Nope. No life. I like it that way. I'm on CoD. The new season is out and trying to complete my battle pass. I'll leave the game I'm in so you can join. Do you still have a mic?

> NOAH14:
>
> Cool. Yeah. I'll connect it now and join you.

A few games in, I realised just how rusty I'd become after not picking up the controller in so long. Of course, Sam sat at the top of the scoreboard on most of the games, all while shouting into his headset.

"So, what's up?" Sam said casually.

"What do you mean?"

"You never come on your Xbox anymore. Especially not since you got with Lola. So, what is it?"

I sighed.

"Yeah. We aren't a thing anymore."

"Shit. Man, I'm sorry. Do you wanna talk about it?"

"Nah, just playing this is good. It's nice to chat to you. We really should do it more." I'd been an awful friend and I'd unintentionally come running to him when my world fell apart. I felt pathetic, but it was exactly what I needed. Sam was there for me without actually being there for me. It was a welcome distraction, an escape from the heart wrenching real world we lived in, and a break I desperately needed to help me feel something other than this overwhelming grief.

CHAPTER 25
LOLA

I'd always been comfortable with silence. The house was often quiet during the holidays with mum and dad working so many hours.

Now, though, the silence was so loud it was deafening. I couldn't bear to listen to music because every song seemed to remind me of him. I couldn't watch my usual films because each one brought back a movie night I'd spent curled up with Noah on the couch. Even the stars reminded me of kissing him under the moon in Cornwall. He was everywhere, and somehow the thought of him was capable of making my entire body ache.

I missed him so much. It had only been a matter of days, but already his absence had torn a gaping hole in my life that I didn't know how to fill. How was it possible that I couldn't remember what I'd done with my life before he'd barrelled into it and lit it up?

I'd done nothing for days, just wandered aimlessly around the house, ignoring my phone and Ollie's knocks at the front door, and trying not to search the internet for information about asexuality.

In the end, the battery on my phone died and I didn't bother to charge it. I didn't want to see anybody after all.

Dave followed me around, whining pitifully. He knew that something was wrong but his usual tricks hadn't made me any better, and he'd never experienced that before. I was going to have to walk him soon, though. Both my parents were on long shifts at work so it was me or nobody, and that wasn't going to be an option. Not if Dave got his own way.

I'd need to have a shower first, though, and wash multiple days worth of moping off myself. My hair was basically one giant mass now, it was so stuck together with grease. Miraculously, the long shower managed to make me feel somewhat more human, and I actually felt able to take Dave out for a walk.

It was a gorgeous day. The winter frost had finally given way to glorious spring weather, and I had to admit that the sunshine did have an impact on my mood. Dave and I headed for the park where he demanded I throw a ball for him until my arm ached and he was panting so hard it looked as though his lolling tongue belonged to another creature entirely.

I was ready to give up and head home when a familiar voice called out to me from across the other side of the park.

"Lola, you're a bloody difficult person to get hold of. Don't you ever read your messages anymore?"

I blinked, shielding my eyes from the sunshine with my hand. The red sunglasses from Cornwall had sat untouched on my desk since I'd come home, where the sight of them made my stomach ache every time I saw them. Hannah stared back at me, also squinting in the bright light.

"Oh, hey," I said dully. "How're you?"

"I'm good. You know everybody is worried about you, right?" Her head tilted sideways as she considered me with interest, her hands reaching down to give Dave the fuss he was demanding by weaving in and out of her legs and slapping his wagging tail against them repeatedly.

"What? Why?"

"Because you haven't answered a single message in days?" she answered as though it was the most obvious thing ever.

"My phone died," I answered with a shrug.

"You see, this is where you would normally use this thing called a charger? They make phones work again so they're not single use. You with me?" She was teasing, but I didn't have it in me to smile.

"Yeah, sorry, I need to do that."

Ducking down to tangle her fingers in Dave's fur while he lost himself in the ecstasy of somebody giving him that amount of attention, she looked at me with narrowed eyes.

"Okay, spill. What's going on?"

"Nothing," I replied unconvincingly. I couldn't even convince myself.

"Uh huh, and I'm the Queen of England. Try again, princess."

I hesitated. "All I ever seem to do is spill my guts whenever you're around. You'll get sick of me. Why don't you tell me about yourself for a change?"

"Because I'm not standing in a park looking like I just lost the winning Euro Millions ticket. And besides, just think of me as your emotional fairy godmother. I'm sure one day I'll need you to return the favour and I'll expect you to jump to it when I do."

That earned a small quiver of my lips. It seemed impossible to think of Hannah as anything other than completely put together and contented. She always seemed so... I don't know... grown up maybe. So much wiser than most people our age.

"Me and Noah broke up," I finally released through a pained sigh.

"Ah," she answered with a long nod of her head and a tone that didn't sound terribly surprised. "I'm sorry to hear that. What happened?"

"I did."

"You *happened*?" she asked, looking genuinely confused.

"Basically." I nodded curtly. I wasn't at all sure I wanted to get into this with her and see the look of triumph on her face when she realised she'd been right all along.

"You're gonna need to give me more than that, honey. Come. Let's sit." Taking my hand, she gave me no choice in the matter, just towed me to the nearest unoccupied bench. She pushed me to sit down then settled in beside me, crossing her legs under her on the bench. "Now, tell me what happened."

"We tried to have sex," I said bluntly. If we were going to do this, it made sense to rip off the plaster right away. "You can go ahead and say I told you so now."

She frowned, no triumph, only sympathy in her expression. "I'm not interested in scoring cheap shots out of people's pain, Lola. I hope I'm not that guy."

Closing my eyes, I groaned, throwing my head back and scrubbing at my cheeks with my hands. "I didn't mean to suggest that you were. I just…" I trailed off, short of words to explain to her how I was feeling.

"So you guys tried to have sex and you weren't into it?" she prompted.

"I froze. I was so sure I could get through it, but I just…."

"Couldn't?"

"Yeah. It wasn't like fear or anything. I just shut down completely. And now he thinks I hate him and I really don't. But he deserves to be with somebody who doesn't think all that stuff is totally abhorrent."

"Does he not get a choice in that?" she asked softly, no judgement in her voice whatsoever. It was a genuine question.

"No teenage boy in their right mind is going to sign up for a life of no sex. It's clear it's what he wants. There were rose petals on the bed, for heaven's sake."

"Oh, he went all out."

"Yep." I ducked my chin to my chest, tears stinging at my eyes once more.

Being without him was awful. I missed him with every heartbeat, but what hurt more than anything else was knowing that I'd broken his heart so badly. "He put on the most perfect, wonderful evening for me, and I ruined it because I'm a freak."

"Hey!" I jerked back slightly when her hand slapped lightly against my leg. "You are *not* a freak. Would you call me that because I like girls?"

"Of course not. There's nothing wrong with liking girls. Hell, I wish I did. It'd be better than this… nothing.

At least you get to settle down one day." And so we came to it—the thought that had been tearing me apart since that moment on the beach when I'd realised that the word Hannah had used on Bonfire Night was actually the one I identified with most.

Asexual.

No sexual attraction.

Utterly repulsed by it, in fact.

"Me?" I went on. "I get to die alone."

She shifted on the bench so her feet landed on the floor and her arm settled over my shoulders, pulling me into her side as the tears that seemed to come so easily these days fell down my cheeks again.

"You don't know that. You need to give yourself some time to adjust to the idea of being ace, but I guarantee it won't always seem like the end of the world like it does now."

I huffed a humourless laugh through my tears, swiping at my wet cheeks in frustration. "I don't see how it can ever feel any better."

She smiled, squeezing me tightly. "It's always darkest right before dawn, right? Just give it some time. I thought the world was ending when I realised I was queer, too, but the sun still continued to rise and set every day and slowly, I started to feel alright with the idea."

"Do you have a girlfriend?" I asked, suddenly ashamed that I had no idea as to the answer.

Her burst of laughter made me jerk back in surprise and she shot me an apologetic smile. "Sorry, it's just that if you'd met my parents, you'd know that the answer to that question is a resounding no."

I blinked and watched her, waiting for her to elaborate, but she didn't.

"What's the deal with your parents?"

"You ever seen The Gilmore Girls?"

"Yeah, course."

"Remember Lorelai's parents?"

My eyes widened. "Oh."

"Yeah, like that but not as rich, way more controlling, and they care ten times more about what people think."

"Ouch," I said, unsure what to do with that information. "So they don't want you to have a girlfriend?"

"Oh, honey," she said, in a way that coming from anybody else would have sounded patronising. "You think I've told them I like girls? Daddy darling still thinks he's going to set me up with a nice boy from the office one day and we'll give him beautiful, perfect grandchildren. I'm not disabusing him of the idea until I'm well and truly moved out and living far, far away."

"Wow, that really sucks. I'm sorry," I said sincerely. The idea of having to hide who I was from my family for fear they wouldn't love me anymore was horrifying. Sure, I wasn't sure how I was going to break my own sexuality to my parents, but I didn't have any fear that they'd give me a hard time over it.

"Eh, it is what it is." She shrugged but the tone of her voice wasn't as dismissive as the words she was trying to make me believe. "Just makes me more excited to go off to uni."

God, uni. I hadn't even given much thought about that next step. I knew I was expected to, but I'd lived in the same place all my life. Somehow, the thought of moving away on my own, to a brand new place where I'd have to start over again with everything, was terrifying. Part of me wanted to just stay put and get a job rather than going through all of that. Either way, it all seemed terribly far into the future still, even though it was only a year and a bit away and the college tutors were always going on about UCAS applications.

"Where do you want to go?" I asked curiously.

"Anywhere away from here would work." She grinned and the light had returned to her eyes now. Clearly, uni was a bright spot on the horizon for her. "Anyway, are you planning on going to the Buzz Fest night at Pockets this weekend? One of the lads from college is singing apparently."

I sighed heavily. The town hosted a music festival every year, showcasing new and unsigned talent from the local area. Noah and I had been planning to go to the night at Pockets together. Now, I wasn't sure I'd be able to stomach it, especially if he was there. "I don't think so," I admitted sadly.

"Well, if you change your mind, call me and we can go together. It might do you good to get out and have some fun."

"Yeah, I will. I'll call you anyway. We should hang out sometime when I'm not having an existential crisis so you can see that I'm not always, in fact, a complete basket case."

When I got home from the park, I finally opened up my laptop and typed a single word into the search bar.

Asexuality.

CHAPTER 26
NOAH

I still hadn't heard from Lola. In fact, all the hope I'd previously clung on to had disappeared. She'd gone silent on the Sandy Crew Whatsapp and I'd finally accepted I wouldn't be seeing her until our return to sixth form.

"Dinner is ready. Do you want me to bring it up?" Mum said through the crack in the door.

After a few days of being solitary with only my Xbox and the sound of Sam's voice keeping me company, I decided it was time to join my parents for an evening meal instead of eating upstairs.

"No, it's okay. I'll be down in a sec," I said to Mum, unmuting my microphone. "Sam, I've got to go. I'll be back on in a bit. Make the zombies pay while I'm gone."

"You've got it."

I followed the scent of mac and cheese downstairs, my mouth watering in anticipation. It would be a welcome change to eating out of necessity.

I sat down and a plate was thrust in front of me with

the creamy pasta piled high. The room remained silent, so quiet I could hear my parents chewing their food, until my dad finally spoke.

"Are you going to Buzz Fest this weekend? Apparently all the different venues around town have drink offers and live music. It's all the rage with kids your age, isn't it?"

I shrugged. I didn't know if I had the energy to put on a brave face in front of my school friends. I was too busy saving that up for the first day back at sixth form.

God, I'm such a loser.

"Maybe. I'm not sure."

"It might lift your spirits a little. You should consider it. Get a group of friends together. I think it's a wonderful idea," Mum chirped in.

"I'll consider it. How are you doing? You know, with your OCD?" My tone made it sound like I was being an arse, but I didn't mean it that way. I did care. In fact, I'd barely seen her for the whole of the Easter holiday so I had no idea how she'd been.

"She's managing," Dad barked, his words straight to the point and coupled with a stern look.

"Are you going to get an appointment at the doctors again? Things seem to have gotten worse, don't you think?" I blurted. It was all true and with my heightened emotions, I couldn't help myself.

"You know that's easier said than done, Noah. You know how hard it is for your mum to set foot in a doctor's surgery. Besides, you know how many times she's tried in the past. There's no help for her. Do you and I need to have a word?"

"It's fine, Ian. It's clearly bothering him." Her face dropped to the floor in sadness. "I'm sorry this is affecting you. It's the thing I hate most about my condition. I hate that it hurts you, your brother and your dad. I wish I could just suffer in silence."

I could see the pain in her expression, how she wished she could take it all away. I wanted to do the same for her, too, but she needed professional help. I could be her emotional support, her loving son, but I was far from being a doctor who might stand a chance of truly helping.

"I don't want you to suffer in silence. I don't want you to suffer *at all*. I'm just saying that maybe there's more help available now than there has been previously. You won't know unless you try. Please, consider going to the doctors. I know it'll be hard but you've got to do it for you. I hate to say this, but if you can't do it for yourself, do it for me."

Mum nodded and agreed that she'd try, but I couldn't help but notice an unconvinced look from Dad. He'd been with Mum every step of the way, helping her manage a condition that had ruled her life for so long, so maybe deep down he didn't believe she could try—maybe he believed she'd given up a long time ago.

The room fell silent, so I tried to break the tension by smiling through a mouthful of mac and cheese, but that smile soon disappeared.

"You might even see Lola at Buzz Fest," Dad said, probably with immediate regret as I felt the table judder as Mum kicked him.

"I doubt it. She's hiding away. Who can blame her?"

I didn't get a reply. Instead, I was met with sympathetic looks from both of them, which were just as bad as the usual 'how are you doing?' and head tilt.

As soon as I finished eating, I kissed my mum on her cheek to say thank you, and hoped she'd consider that an apology without me actually saying sorry for being so forthcoming, then rushed back upstairs to kill more zombies with Sam.

"Back. What did I miss?"

"I managed to kill a few zombies in the inner circle before ex-filling. Shall we give it a try together?"

"Sure, but if I'm rubbish, you're gonna have to protect me."

I was just met with chuckles from Sam, who set up the game for us to join.

"Are you going to Buzz Fest this weekend?" I asked him.

"Dunno. Forgot it was on to be honest. Is that why they're mentioning Pockets in the Sandy Crew chat?"

"Oh, maybe. Do you fancy going with me? As much as I've enjoyed not having to deal with people for a while, I think it might be good for me."

"Yeah. What if Lola is out, though? Won't that be awkward?"

"Probably, but I've got to see her sometime, haven't I? Think I'd prefer it to be when I have easy access to alcohol, and they frown upon that at sixth form."

"Fair play. Yeah, go on then. Now, pay attention otherwise you'll get me killed," Sam said while shooting a large ray gun at a large lizard-like creature. "BOOM!"

———

Sam and I walked up the steps into Pockets. I'd never seen the place so busy. The whole town was buzzing in fact, to the point where we had to queue to get in.

I caught a glimpse of myself in the mirrors that lined

the stairs while we waited and checked my appearance just in case I were to run into Lola. Picking an outfit for that evening had turned out to be harder than our first date. I couldn't wear my pale blue shirt; I didn't think I'd ever be able to again, and I certainly couldn't wear red—I'd never be able to unsee how cute she'd looked in those stupid bright red sunglasses.

Once inside, we could barely make it to the bar. It was so crowded I wouldn't have been able to find Lola even if I tried—she hadn't got the nickname Lola-Little-Legs for no reason.

I ordered two vodka and Cokes, because who could refuse a deal? I poured them into the one glass before Sam and I fought our way through the crowd to face the singer—the one who was singing all about love.

I knew this was a bad idea.

I glugged down a large mouthful of my drink and tried to disguise my expression of disgust at the strong taste as it burned its way down my throat.

I couldn't help but allow my eyes to wander around the venue. I even spotted Ollie and Cade over at the bar doing colourful shots together, which made me wonder if Lola wasn't far off.

I battled my way to the bar just a couple of people away from them and waited to order another drink. Right on cue, they spotted me.

"That's Noah. Noah?" I heard them say and then turned to face them.

"Oh, hey, guys. Are you having fun?" I asked, and the two strangers in between us made a space through so I could get closer to Ollie and Cade.

"Yeah. Who knew Pockets could be this busy?" Cade

said, downing another shot and passing me a brightly coloured red one that was lined up on the bar.

"I know right. I was just saying the same to Sam."

"Oh, Sam's here? That's not like him. He barely leaves his room usually, right?" Ollie said with a smirk and clinked his shot glass with mine. "Cheers! Oh my god, let's have a picture."

Before I knew it, I was smiling into his phone camera and my eyes were blinded by the bright flash as he took the photo.

"So, where's Lola?" I asked nervously, the alcohol intensifying the butterflies in my stomach.

"Your guess is as good as mine to be honest," Ollie replied with a shrug that I suspected was meant to be nonchalant but absolutely wasn't. "She doesn't tell me shit these days."

"Ah. I thought she might have come with you, that's all."

"Sorry, man. As far as I know, she's not here. I heard you guys split. That's grim. I'm so sorry."

Ollie knew. That must mean Lola had reached out to someone. It made me feel physically sick hearing out loud that Lola and I were a nothing.

"How do you know?" I asked as the waitress asked me what I'd like to drink. I ordered two more vodka and Cokes.

"Good question. There was a time when she would have told me herself but she isn't replying to my messages or answering the door to me these days. I heard it third hand through Cade who heard it from Hannah. Apparently, they met in the park and Lola actually spoke to her. Wonder of wonders." He rolled his eyes and I got the impression he was kinda frustrated with her. I wanted to tell him how distraught Lola had been on that beach in Cornwall, but it didn't feel like my place.

"Sorry. I should have messaged to tell you. I know you and Lola are best mates, but I hope that we can still be friends. Anyway, I'll leave you guys to have a good night. I'll go find Sam."

"Absolutely, don't be a stranger, will you?" Ollie called after me as I walked away with my drinks after smiling in their direction.

A different band got up on stage whose music was a little heavier than I was used to. Pockets began to empty of the few familiar faces and new ones came in, taking up space on the newly created dance floor since all the tables and chairs had been stacked up to make space.

Sam and I put up with the new music, but only because the drinks were far too good value to go anywhere else. The band did seem to get better the more I drank.

"Fancy another drink?" I yelled to Sam above the music.

"Another? You're out of control. I'm good, but I'll come to the bar with you. I don't exactly fit in with this crowd."

I turned towards the bar, but instead of focusing on the very nice waitress who had illegally been plying me with alcohol all night, I saw Ollie and Cade looking bothered.

An older pair of lads stood a few feet away, pointing and laughing at my friends——at Lola's friends.

"Are you guys alright?" I asked after walking over to them. Before either of them could answer, I understood they were absolutely not okay.

"Look at those gay boys. Disgusting queers."

I felt instantly sick for both of them. I couldn't imagine

how they must have felt, having to deal with so much hate for just being who they were——for being good people.

"You're both ignorant, cave dwelling pigs. Leave us alone," Cade yelled, but as one of the lads jumped forward in what can only be described as a standoff in the wilderness, Cade's confidence soon disappeared.

"They probably want to fuck us." The strangers laughed, their comment forcing Ollie to stand in front of Cade to protect him.

The same lad lunged forward again, this time pushing Ollie backwards into Cade, who slid against the edge of the bar and onto the floor.

Without thought, I jumped in front of Ollie. The lad was the same size as me, and although I hadn't been in a fight since year eight, I considered punching the lighthouse wall as practice for taking down at least one of the uneducated bullies in front of me.

"What the fuck are you guys playing at? They aren't bothering anyone," I said, huffing a breath, trying to hide my nerves as I protected the one guy I knew Lola would do anything for. His narrowed eyes were locked on mine and his face was so close I could feel his stale breath.

I tried to be nice.

I tried to de-escalate the situation.

But he didn't help me do that. Instead, he laughed in my face.

I balled a fist and launched it against his jaw the minute he broke eye contact. He stumbled, but quickly regained balance and shoved into me, pushing all of us backward and attracting the attention of the bar staff.

Once I managed to compose myself, I hit him angrily, grunting out words with every contact.

"Homophobic. Bastards." I took a breath. "This. Is. For. Lola."

I saw red—an angry red, similar to the colour of Lola's sunglasses.

But I couldn't keep up the momentum, and as the other lad joined in, they knocked me to the floor and began kicking the air right out of me.

I didn't know how long it lasted.

I didn't even remember people trying to break us up.

Everything was dark, pitch black, like I was in the middle of the ocean with nothing and nobody to rescue me.

All I could hear was the howling of sirens and deep voices that echoed in my ears until even they faded out.

CHAPTER 27
LOLA

I shouldn't have looked at my phone. It was pretty much always a mistake to look at social media, even when your life was going well. But looking when everything had fallen spectacularly apart, *and* on a night when half the people you knew were going to be out having a blast was downright masochistic.

Snapchat was full of people from college enjoying the Buzz Fest night at Pockets. Every photo and video made my stomach sink while searching every millimetre of the background for that face I knew would hurt more than any other.

I was sure Noah would have gone. He was much more naturally sociable than me so likely wouldn't be able to resist. Still, I couldn't find him in anybody's photos and I couldn't look at his own snaps. That would definitely shatter what was left of my heart.

And then Ollie posted a story and I made the mistake of opening it, assuming it would be the usual lovey-dovey crap he posted daily of him and Cade. Sure enough, he was there, and so was Cade, but there, right in the middle of the two of them, smiling in a totally unconvincing way, was Noah.

He looked so tired, defeated even. He had dark circles under his eyes, and the light that usually shone so brightly in his smile was absent. God, I'd done that to him. Guilt hit me like a wrecking ball and my stomach twisted painfully. I'd loved him so much—still did if I were being honest—and the sight of him so obviously hurting broke me in two all over again.

Shutting the app down, I tossed my phone to the end of the bed where it was out of reach. I didn't want to torture myself anymore, but it was only a matter of minutes before it was back in my hand and I was watching for Ollie and Cade's names like a hawk. They didn't post again, though, and eventually, I stopped watching and occupied myself with attempting to focus on the coursework I'd ignored all holiday in favour of moping around and feeling generally sorry for myself.

After nights of broken sleep, the soporific effect of college work didn't take long to kick in, and I felt my eyes drooping relentlessly, my head dipping to the desktop and resting there.

I wasn't sure if it was minutes or hours later when the shrill ringing of my phone broke through my sleep and I woke up with a start. It took me several seconds to work out where I was and what was happening before I was able to process enough to reach for my phone and stare blearily at the screen.

Ollie was calling me. It had been ages since he'd called. He knew I didn't use my phone to make actual calls. It was strictly a texting device. So why was he calling me from a night out? It didn't make any sense.

"Hello?" I said warily after swiping to answer his call.

"Dudette, whatever is going on between you and Noah, you need to suck it up and get here now."

"What do you mean?" I replied sharply, bristling.

"That hero has just stood up for us, Lolz. He's in hospital and he needs you."

The entire world fell out through my stomach as my vision flickered with black around the edges. Three words repeated over and over in my mind while Ollie carried on talking, completely unheard by me.

Noah.

Hero.

Hospital.

Noah.

Hero.

Hospital.

The words swirled around in my mind as I fought to make sense of anything Ollie was saying.

Noah was fine. I'd seen him only a short time ago in that picture. Sure, he looked done-in and depressed, but not like he needed a hospital.

"Ollie," I whispered, but he kept talking in words I couldn't make any sense of. "Ollie!" I repeated louder and more forcefully, and this time he stopped talking. "I need you to slow down and tell me again. I'm lost."

"Just get here, Lolz. He's in a bad way. I know you care about him no matter what's happened between you, so please. Just get here now."

"Where is he?"

"St. Jude's."

"I'm on my way."

Panic buzzed through my system, zinging around every one of my nerves and making my hands shake as I tried to call a taxi on a phone which seemed to have turned to jelly.

My heart was a fist punching at my ribs in an attempt to break free of my chest as we pulled up outside the well lit hospital reception. I fumbled through paying the driver, who had talked to me for the entire drive without me hearing a single word, then stepped outside and stared up at the foreboding building in front of me.

How many times had I worried about him when he'd been surfing? I'd convinced myself over and over that he was going to be eaten by a shark, or crash against the rocks, or get swept out to sea where he'd be lost forever. And now, he'd somehow been hurt on an innocent night out with his friends. It didn't make any sense, and I needed answers.

Forcing one foot in front of the other, I made my way inside where the fluorescent lights made my eyes swim and my head ache. I was making for the reception counter when I heard Ollie's voice calling my name behind me. Peering over my shoulder, I saw him just in time before he collided with me and swept me into a tighter hug than I could ever remember experiencing from him before. Inhaling deeply and taking in his old familiar and reassuring scent, I squeezed him right back before pulling back to find out what had happened to land Noah in hospital of all places.

"He was amazing, Lolz. These guys were giving Cade and me grief, and he just stepped in and tried to get them to back off."

Of course he did. Noah could never stand to see anybody being mistreated, especially people he cared about.

"I'm assuming since he's landed himself in hospital that he wasn't successful?"

"He's pretty beaten up but the doctors say it's all superficial. They're doing X-rays and scans to be sure but they think he'll be fine."

Relief swept over me like a tidal wave and if Ollie hadn't been there to steady me, I would likely have fallen to my knees right there in the waiting room.

"When can we see him?"

It would be awkward but I needed to see for myself that he was okay.

"They said they'll let us know."

The waiting room was busy so I distracted myself from my worry by people watching and imagining why each person was there. After a short time, Nate also arrived looking frantic and worried. After a short conversation with the man behind the reception desk, he came and sat beside us, joining our silent vigil.

Seconds felt like minutes and minutes felt like hours as we waited for somebody—anybody—to come and tell us something. The hands on the clinical white clock on the wall moved stubbornly slowly until a kind looking woman with a stethoscope around her neck came over to speak to us.

She used long, scary sounding words but the crux of the matter seemed to be that he had a couple of broken ribs and a lot of cuts and bruising, but on the whole, it looked a lot worse than it was. Medically, at least.

Since he was family, Nate was invited through to see

him first, and it was torture waiting for him to return and tell us what to expect. Ollie sat patiently beside me the whole time, his hand periodically squeezing my shoulder or knee in either sympathy or solidarity. A few times I thought he was going to say something. I knew he must have had questions about what was going on with me.

In the end, I saved him the job, twisting in my seat and biting my lip as I fought to find the words.

It was all wrong, feeling so tongue tied and awkward around my best friend in the world. I'd always assumed that we'd be best friends until we were old and causing chaos in the same nursing home together. Yet, recently, we'd somehow drifted apart and I hated that.

"Thank you for calling me tonight, Ol," I started cautiously.

He huffed a laugh with no humour in it, glancing at me before looking back down at his hands. "I was surprised when you answered if I'm being honest."

My head dipped on my shoulders, shame filling me at how I'd treated him—treated everybody who'd tried to contact me lately.

"I'm sorry I've been so... flakey. I didn't know how to be around anybody."

"So you shut yourself off. After everything we've been through together, you still thought isolating yourself was a good idea?" He looked back up at me, eyebrows raised and expression fierce.

He had a point.

"I didn't mean..."

"That was my favourite coping strategy once upon a time, Lolz, and I think we can agree it didn't work out well for anybody."

There was no answer I could give to that to exonerate myself of my hypocrisy after giving him so much grief over and over for self isolating when he was struggling with his mental health. All I could do was nod, my eyes fixed on my twisting hands in my lap.

"You can talk to me, you know?" he went on. "I know you think I'm too busy with Cade, but I will never be too busy to make time for you. You're my best friend and I have no idea what's going on with you. The last time we talked seriously, you said something about grappling with your sexuality, then the next thing I know you have a boyfriend. So I guess you figured that out?"

Sighing, I tried to clear my head by massaging my temples, but Ollie took hold of my hands and held them between us, looking me dead in the eye with the most earnest expression I'd ever seen on his face.

"Tell me, Lolz. Whatever it is that's making you so sad, tell me about it."

"I'm not gay," I said softly. "I wish I was. At least then I'd stand a chance of finding somebody to be with."

"I don't follow," he replied, clearly confused.

"I'm asexual, Ol," I said quickly. The word sounded strange and foreign on my tongue, but as I said it aloud for the first time to somebody else, something inside me slotted into place, and I knew that it was right.

He inhaled sharply and I tried to pull my hands back, but his grip tightened and the most beautiful smile slowly spread onto his face.

"Actually, that makes a lot of sense."

Then two arms closed around me and I fell headfirst into the most familiar of all hugs, clutching my best friend tight and feeling all our love for one another in that tight ring of friendship.

Eventually, Nate returned and looked directly at me.

"He's asking for you. I told him you were here."

"Is he... okay?" I asked, knowing it was a stupid question, but the fear of not knowing what I'd see when I walked in to see him was killing me.

"He's Noah," he said in a tone that was probably meant to be reassuring but really wasn't.

He showed me through to a cubicle surrounded by a starchy, pale blue curtain. The air all around smelled of antiseptic and illness. Sharply, I was reminded of the day we'd almost lost Ollie in this very same hospital.

Was I destined to always let people down?

Nudging the privacy curtain aside, I peered through the gap to see Noah sitting upright in the bed. His face was a patchwork of bruises and cuts, and behind all the injuries, I could tell that he was as pale as a ghost.

"Hey," I whispered, shuffling forward to the bedside and offering him a timid smile.

"Hey, Little-Legs," Noah croaked, coughing a little and wincing through his speech.

Awkwardness forgotten, I shot forward in concern, my hands waving uselessly around, afraid to touch him anywhere in case I hurt him. "Oh god, Noah. Are you okay?"

It was a stupid question, but of all the million and one things I needed to say to him, those were the words that fell out.

"Never felt better if I'm honest," he said, smirking

through the pain. His hand moved closer to me, sliding down the bed, but then he hesitated. It seemed he was too afraid to touch me, too.

"Acting as shark bait wasn't enough for you? You had to bait the local bigots, too?" The words erupted from me through a sob I had no control over.

"Well, that wasn't my initial plan for the evening. It just sorta happened. I couldn't bear seeing Ollie and Cade deal with those homophobic bullies. Think I might have ended up worse off, though."

"You're an idiot, Noah Larson. But god, you're a brave idiot."

You're my idiot… The words rose and died on my tongue because he wasn't mine anymore. He never could be again. But god I wanted to kiss him, to hold him and never let him do anything stupid and dangerous ever again.

"I don't feel very brave right now." He sucked a breath in through his teeth as he moved a little to get comfortable. "I'm glad you came, though. I know I've said it so many times, but I really am sorry."

My hands fluttered helplessly at the sight of his pain but settled on the bed rail. "What in god's name are you sorry for? You did nothing wrong."

"I'm sorry for lots of things. I'm sorry for making you come to the hospital at god knows what hour. I'm sorry I didn't get better shots when punching the lads who thought it was okay to single out friends for just being themselves, but most of all," he paused, catching his breath. I saw his fingers move a little towards me, like they were trying to reach out for me. "I'm sorry I pushed you away. I'm sorry for wanting more with you, but I couldn't help myself. I... I..." The words seemed to be caught in his throat.

"Oh, Noah." My hand shifted ever so slightly to land lightly on top of his. "You didn't push me away. This is all me. You did nothing wrong. Nothing. If anything, I'm flattered that you wanted more with me. I just wish I could give it to you."

Another sob cut free from my chest and I lifted my free hand to swipe away the tears that fell so easily these days.

"I don't need it. I just need you. What's up, Little-Legs?"

My head dipped, my loose hair swinging forward to cover my face. I couldn't look him in the eye and tell him what I'd learned about myself that night in Cornwall.

"Everything was perfect. I loved you... *love* you so much. I adored every second with you until..." I hesitated, the words choking off with the realisation that once they were out there, he'd finally be utterly out of reach to me.

"You love me? You still love me?" His eyes brightened, looking a clear blue next to the bruises and cuts on his face. "That's all I'll ever need. You."

"I'm not right though, Noah. I can't give you what you need and I never will be able to. I... I'm asexual." The final words were whispered so quietly I was almost certain he wouldn't be able to hear, but when his eyes widened, it seemed that he had.

"What does that mean?" He sat up a little more. His hand turned to link with mine, his fingers slotting perfectly into the gaps between mine. One of his fingers softly grazed the back of my hand, sending sensations both physical and emotional fizzing through me.

"It means that while I love you so much it's like a physical pain, I'm never going to be okay with sleeping with you. No matter how much I wish I could give you that."

Noah's head fell back and looked to the ceiling. For a minute, it confirmed my worries. Noah Larson wanted to have sex. It was natural, and I couldn't blame him for that. He looked back to me after what felt like an eternity and said, "If sex is the only thing that's off the cards and loving you isn't, if this is the only thing that you're worried about not being able to give me, then why are you not already in my arms? Yeah, sex with you would be nice," he said a little quieter, as if to stop his brother from hearing on the other side of the curtain. "But I'd rather have no sex if it means we can be together. Think of the memories. Think of the kisses, Lola. Wait... we can still kiss, right?"

I laughed through the tears that were still falling. "Yes, we can still kiss. Every asexual is different. Some don't even like kissing, but kissing you is... everything. But, Noah, you don't understand. This isn't going to change. I'm not gonna turn around one day and change my mind. At least I don't think so. My research didn't get me that far. We're only seventeen. You can't possibly say now that you'll always be happy without sex."

"I can. Let me be okay with this Lola. Let yourself be okay with this. I love you, Little-Legs. Let me love you for who you are. All I want right now is for you to love me back." His eyelids had puddled with tears and his voice cracked through the pain, physical and emotional.

"But... how can you say that you're always going to be okay with it? How can you know you're not going to turn around one day in the future and decide you've had enough?"

Noah paused. The room went almost silent, the only

noise the low bleeping from nearby hospital monitors. "I don't know. I really don't know. The only thing I do know is that every day I spend with you, I fall for you a little more. I couldn't picture being with anyone else. I don't want to be standing next to anyone other than you when we graduate. I don't want to go surfing without your incessant nagging that I'm going to be eaten by a shark. I want you. Let me want you. I promise I won't hurt you."

Every word hit me with the force of a ten tonne truck and I openly sobbed with so many emotions flooding through me all at once. I wanted so badly to be with him, to trust that this could work. Everything in me cried out for him and I couldn't help but lean closer and press my lips to his. He winced slightly, but when I tried to pull away, his hand shifted to the back of my head and nudged me closer again.

Our foreheads connected as I breathed against his lips, "I love you so much. I'm just so afraid of not being enough for you."

"You're enough. Every single one of your five feet is perfect. You don't have to be afraid. We should be excited."

His face was so earnest, so filled with love as I pulled back to look at him that my entire body filled with warmth.

"I am excited. Excited to spend more weekends worrying about you getting eaten by sharks." I grinned through the sheen of tears still lingering on my cheeks. "Or taking on the town bigots, of course."

"I think it's time I retire my bigot fighting ways for a while, but I'm sure it won't be too long before I'm well enough to go surfing again. What do you say... fancy giving Cornwall another try?"

"I love Cornwall. I'll sit on the beach with a good book and a pasty and you can fight off the local sea monsters." I grinned, wishing I could hug him without hurting him.

"A book and a pasty on the beach sounds good. Come here." Noah pulled me into him, embracing me and the pain, and I felt whole for the first time since that awful night in Cornwall. "For the record, I've now been hurt way more on dry land than I ever have in the water. I think we will be safer out in the open ocean. Is this a good time to tell you I want to live on a boat?" He laughed, his smile bright enough to guide a hundred ships back to shore in the dead of night.

I slapped him lightly on the arm, ignoring his feigned wince. "Like I said: you're an idiot. But you're my idiot, Shark Boy."

EPILOGUE

NOAH - A FEW MONTHS LATER...

At the start of sixth form, not once had I believed I'd end up coming on holiday to Cornwall with Lola, never mind with both our families and a few of our friends. But there we were, soaking up the sun. A few of us sunbathed while Ollie, Cade, Lola and her dog, Dave, frolicked about in the water. It was good to see Lola comfortable enough to be up to her knees in the ocean, considering the last time we'd been there, she'd been all for remaining on dry land. This time, I didn't even have to coach her in. In fact, it was Dave who ran straight towards the ocean in excitement and Lola chased after him without hesitation. Dave kicked his little doggie legs so hard around them, he created a spray of salty water that splashed Lola in the face, washing away her smile and replacing it with that oh so familiar look of distaste of the water.

I stayed on the beach, close to both mine and Lola's parents who were sipping coffee together, because 'hot drinks really do cool you down'. I laughed and considered it the adults' way to keep their caffeine addictions up in summer without judgement.

My brother and Emma were sitting next to me. At the start of the month, they had announced their engagement and they planned to marry soon. It was a little quick if you asked me, but there was no doubt that Emma was the best thing for Nate since his acne medication, and I knew their happiness was the same as mine and Lola's. If you were to bottle them both up, they'd have the same ingredients.

My heart filled with warmth as everyone important to me were on that beach with me, well, aside from Sam. Selfishly, I wished he'd come along, but since that night in Pockets, he'd barely left his room for anything other than sixth form.

He'd escaped from Pockets physically unscathed, but I could see that night had affected him in another way. He was more reclusive, more Sam-like than ever before.

I couldn't help but smile at the thought of Sam at the beach with us. No doubt he'd have been slathered in sunscreen, locked underneath a parasol and glued to his phone. It would have been his worst nightmare.

In just short of a week, I'd be back home, where we could play together on our games consoles. I'd learnt to appreciate the peace and tranquillity of being indoors. Sam had helped me to understand that when my world turned dystopian, games could be my escape. Maybe that was why he played so much.

I wiped my face, trying to clear it of the sweat, sea water and sand that had clung to it after our walk to the beach. The summer sun was shining in all of its glory, the start of a heatwave, and I couldn't get enough of it.

Of course, Lola was covered in layer upon layer of

factor fifty sunscreen. She didn't tan; she just went bright red—the same colour as my cheeks the first time we'd kissed and close to the bright red of her sunglasses.

She looked beautiful in those glasses. Well, she looked beautiful even without them, even straight out of bed with her hair in knots and her pyjamas ridden up. I'd had the pleasure of witnessing the grumpy delights of morning Lola on this trip, as we slept in the same bed.

It was the first time we'd been in a bed together since our Easter holiday, which hadn't ended well. I'd been a little apprehensive about the whole thing and I was sure Lola was, too, but it had turned out to be the most amazing night.

I held her in my arms for hours on end, watching her nod off as I stroked her hair until we both fell asleep.

The reality of our relationship and the boundaries we'd put in place didn't faze me, because I had Lola. The way she made my heart swell and how bright her smile made me feel along with how often she made me laugh were things I wasn't willing to give up. To ask for more? I'd have been trading off everything I loved about her. How could I ask her to be anyone but herself—to give me something she couldn't give—when what I had was perfect enough already?

"Hey, Little-Legs," I yelled from the shore, prompting a smile from her parents. "Is it time to play one of the beach games yet?"

"As long as it involves me going no further into the water, you're on." Lola rounded up Dave, who continued to splash around her, and Ollie and Cade followed, holding hands as they emerged from the water.

I began setting up a rounders game with my brother,

who had recently taken charge of the team at Allerton and was pretty clued up on the rules. I, however, hadn't played since I was in year seven. The teams were split, teens on one team, the oldies on the other, with Nate joining our team and Emma with the parents.

Nate bowled under arm to Emma, and with a mighty swing of her bat, she missed. She ran and made it to first base but after a lot of discussion, it was decided she was out because she threw the bat on the floor. Emma took herself off to the sidelines, sat down, opened her book and grinned. She was far too clever for her own good.

Up next, my mum. Her daisy patterned summer dress floated effortlessly in the wind as she positioned herself to bat. Her eyes were glued to the ball with determination. The ball was bowled and with the power of Mum's swing, the ball became a blur of yellow as it shot across the sky and down the beach. We ran after it, even Dave who must have thought we were playing the game for him.

Nate grabbed the ball and began running to the posts and my attention turned to Mum, who was holding her dress and running for dear life, with the biggest smile I'd ever seen her wear as she was cheered on by the other parents.

I couldn't help but cheer her on, too. She'd been through a lot. We all had. Mum had since managed to go to the doctors to get a little more help and support. She'd told me the final nail in the coffin was when she found out I'd been taken to hospital. At the news, the comfort she found in routine was shattered and the thought of stepping inside a hospital with the germs and disease sent her into a huge mental spiral. That was why Nate had been there and not my parents. It had hurt at the time, but I'd also learnt that it hurt them just as much.

Mum would always have OCD. It would never go away, even with medication and therapy. There was no cure. But in the short few months since she'd started treatment, I'd seen it give her a new lease of life. In fact, she'd given that to all of us.

Nate barely made it to the third post just as Mum hit the fourth. Everyone cheered except for Nate, who began screaming at our team like he would at Allerton.

"Come on, guys! Don't tell me I've picked the wrong team."

Lola walked by me, laughing at Nate's serious expression. "What's up with him? It's only a bit of fun."

"You should know by now that games in the Larson household are never fun. They're competitive and relationship destroying. Do you not remember the Monopoly incident a few Mondays ago when you joined us for our family tea? We're still finding little green houses around the dining room."

To Nate's frustration, we didn't win the rounders. The parents beat us by a landslide, so Lola and I took that as our cue to go for a walk with Ollie and Cade, away from the competitive vein popping in Nate's head.

Our hands barely separated and I kissed Lola over and over. I loved that she wanted to kiss me just as much as I wanted to kiss her.

We walked past the very shop where Lola had bought her bright red sunglasses, which prompted each of us to buy a different coloured pair so we could all match. We looked as though we'd formed a budget band in the naughties.

"Hannah's just messaged. She says she misses us. I still can't believe she wasn't allowed to come," Cade said, tapping away at his phone in the middle of the shop while wearing his new bright blue sunglasses.

"I know. I really miss her. I feel like the gang is incomplete without her. Do we even know why she's grounded?" Lola said, posing in a mirror with Ollie.

"Nope. I don't even think she knows herself if I'm honest. It's those parents of hers. Let's go get ice cream, head down to the beach and write a message to her in the sand. She'll love that."

At Cade's suggestion, we headed out of the shop, but Lola's attention turned to a spinning rack holding colourful plaques just outside the entrance. Some had funny sayings on and the others were engraved with inspirational quotes. We spent a few moments giggling to ourselves before seeing one that prompted Lola to wrap her arms around me.

"Happiness is not about getting all that you want. It is about enjoying all that you have."

I read it aloud before my lips met Lola's without hesitation. She tasted like ocean spray and raspberry lip balm and smelt of sandy beaches, just like the one we'd grown to love together.

"I love you, Little-Legs. Everything about you."

"Not as much as I love you, Shark Boy."

The sun had begun its descent towards the horizon while we enjoyed ice cream, wrote messages in the sand and splashed in the calm ocean.

I discreetly bobbed my head underwater, looking out into the deep blue. I couldn't see any sharks or sea monsters—there was nothing deadly around us. All I could see was Lola's little legs fighting to keep the rest of her afloat while holding onto the noodle she'd insisted on bringing for dear life.

I grabbed her leg and began pulling her into the water. Feeling her resistance, I heard muffled screams as my ears were filled with sea water and then popped up out of the water.

"Noah Larson, I am going to kill you! I thought you were a shark." Lola's hand glided along the top of the water, sending a wave cascading in my direction.

"I'm just living up to my nickname." I winked. "Besides, there are no sharks. I've just checked."

"Good, because if I do get eaten by a shark, you'll be sorry. I'll haunt you with the words 'I told you so' for the rest of your life."

I chuckled, paddling closer to her, my arms coming to her sides as we floated together underneath the slowly changing hues of orange and pink that lit up the horizon as the sun set.

With a gentle kiss, I looked into her eyes that glistened so much I could have danced underneath them, and whispered, "I wouldn't expect anything less."

THE END

ALSO BY D J COOK

Light Me Up Series

When Our Worlds Collide

The TLC Series

Tamsin

Liam

Book 3 - Coming soon

Standalones

Finding Fleur

ALSO BY H.A. ROBINSON

Light Me Up Series

When Our Worlds Collide

The Colwich Lake Series

The Pebble Jar

Chasing The Sunrise

Butterfly Kisses

Standalones

The Rarest Rose

To Where You Are

Learning To Fall

Printed in Great Britain
by Amazon